Niagara Falls
& Other Plays

Steve Yockey

GW00645527

A SAMUEL FRENCH ACTING EDITION

FOUNDED 1830

SAMUELFRENCH.COM
SAMUELFRENCH-LONDON.CO.UK

Copyright © 2015 by Steve Yockey
All Rights Reserved
Cover Art Design by Huntley Woods

NIAGARA FALLS & OTHER PLAYS is fully protected under the copyright laws of the United States of America, the British Commonwealth, including Canada, and all other countries of the Copyright Union. All rights, including professional and amateur stage productions, recitation, lecturing, public reading, motion picture, radio broadcasting, television and the rights of translation into foreign languages are strictly reserved.

ISBN 978-0-573-70458-1

www.SamuelFrench.com
www.SamuelFrench-London.co.uk

FOR PRODUCTION ENQUIRIES

UNITED STATES AND CANADA
Info@SamuelFrench.com
1-866-598-8449

UNITED KINGDOM AND EUROPE
Plays@SamuelFrench-London.co.uk
020-7255-4302

Each title is subject to availability from Samuel French, depending upon country of performance. Please be aware that NIAGARA FALLS & OTHER PLAYS may not be licensed by Samuel French in your territory. Professional and amateur producers should contact the nearest Samuel French office or licensing partner to verify availability.

CAUTION: Professional and amateur producers are hereby warned that NIAGARA FALLS & OTHER PLAYS is subject to a licensing fee. Publication of this play(s) does not imply availability for performance. Both amateurs and professionals considering a production are strongly advised to apply to Samuel French before starting rehearsals, advertising, or booking a theatre. A licensing fee must be paid whether the title(s) is presented for charity or gain and whether or not admission is charged. Professional/Stock licensing fees are quoted upon application to Samuel French.

No one shall make any changes in this title(s) for the purpose of production. No part of this book may be reproduced, stored in a retrieval system, or transmitted in any form, by any means, now known or yet to be invented, including mechanical, electronic, photocopying, recording, videotaping, or otherwise, without the prior written permission of the publisher. No one shall upload this title(s), or part of this title(s), to any social media websites.

For all enquiries regarding motion picture, television, and other media rights, please contact Samuel French.

MUSIC USE NOTE

Licensees are solely responsible for obtaining formal written permission from copyright owners to use copyrighted music in the performance of this play and are strongly cautioned to do so. If no such permission is obtained by the licensee, then the licensee must use only original music that the licensee owns and controls. Licensees are solely responsible and liable for all music clearances and shall indemnify the copyright owners of the play(s) and their licensing agent, Samuel French, against any costs, expenses, losses and liabilities arising from the use of music by licensees. Please contact the appropriate music licensing authority in your territory for the rights to any incidental music.

IMPORTANT BILLING AND CREDIT REQUIREMENTS

If you have obtained performance rights to this title, please refer to your licensing agreement for important billing and credit requirements.

TABLE OF CONTENTS

Skulls

SKULLS was commissioned and produced by Chalk Repertory Theatre in Los Angeles, California. It premiered at the Page Museum at the La Brea Tar Pits as a part of *Flash Festival 2012* on September 15, 2012. The production was directed by Abigail Deser. The cast was as follows:

JESS ....Katie Skelton

MATTHEW .... Andrew Crabtree

CHARACTERS

JESS – a woman
MATTHEW – a man

AUTHOR'S NOTES

[ ] in the script indicate overlapping dialogue.

The entire play takes place in the pass-through area between the wall of Dire Wolf skulls and the Dire Wolf display cabinet in the Page Museum.

(**JESS** *stands in front of a massive wall of Dire Wolf skulls. They are backlit with orange light. She looks like the morning after.* **MATT** *enters looking around.* **JESS** *moves further down the wall, trying not to be seen. But* **MATT** *spots her.*)

MATT. Oh, hey. Hey. You're here.

(She smiles awkwardly but doesn't really engage.)

Buy you a coffee?

JESS. It's a museum.

MATT. I'm sure they have caffeine here [somewhere.]

JESS. [I'm good.] What are you doing here?

MATT. You said you were coming today and I said I'd come with you.

JESS. Oh, I thought you were just being polite.

MATT. Nope, I've never been here before.

JESS. I remember you said that. Right after I said I've never been here before. And right before you said you hate museums.

MATT. Well this museum has animatronic animals killing each other.

JESS. In slow motion.

MATT. Still, that's a plus.

JESS. How do you even know that; I thought you've never been here?

MATT. I've already done a lap around the place, I didn't see you the first time. Or the second time.

JESS. I was hiding. I thought you'd give up.

MATT. Uh huh.

JESS. No, I really was hiding.

MATT. So anyway, you were gone when I woke up this morning and that meant I didn't have a chance [to say...]

JESS. [Oh, that's what] we're doing, we're talking about it? Because I was hoping we could do the other thing. Not talk about it. Ever. Like it didn't happen, [like that.]

MATT. [Oh no, it] absolutely happened, Jess.

JESS. I'm trying to, don't make a scene while I'm looking at...wolf skulls. It didn't happen.

MATT. That's funny because I was there and you were there and it happened.

JESS. That's funny because this is the opposite of what I just said I wanted which was, *again*, to never talk about it.

MATT. Well, I guess I'm sorry, but we have to talk about it.

JESS. This doesn't look like four hundred wolf skulls, does it?

> *(She begins to count the wolf skulls. Individually. He waits a moment to feel out if she's seriously going to count them all. It appears she is, so...)*

MATT. Just count across and then up and multiply. And last night totally happened.

JESS. Well, it shouldn't have. And keep your voice down. You're one of my best friends. Friends. That's what you are and it's what you will be in the foreseeable future as long as we don't have to talk about what may or may not have happened last night. When we were both drunk.

MATT. Only kind of drunk.

JESS. Ugh.

MATT. Don't make that face, it was great. It was great, right? I understand it's an odd turn for our friendship, but why would we pretend not to, no, you know what? It was great. And we should fully do it again. A lot. I think we should make it a competitive [sport, I mean...]

JESS. [Under no] circumstances.

MATT. Jess.

JESS. Ugh, don't say my name like that, like I'm a little kid and you know what I'm doing, because you don't know what [I'm doing.]

MATT. [I do know] what you're doing; you're my best friend.

JESS. Emphasis on "friend." And I'm not talking about this. In front of other people. Strange people. And dead things. You wouldn't think this many wolves could just wander into the tar pit.

MATT. They don't "just wander into the tar pit," didn't you watch the little movie? In the tiny auditorium [over there?]

JESS. [Yes. I know] that, I saw it. I was obviously making conversation that doesn't have to do with us engaging in the mistake we made last night. Mistake. Wait, you sat and watched the movie? Jesus, how long have you been here?

MATT. I got curious on my second lap. You know I'm a curious person.

JESS. Right. Well, it's a pretty big place, so if you wanna go check out any of the other exhibits you should absolutely go away and do that.

MATT. Look, Jess…

(He takes her hands. She looks around awkwardly like she might bolt.)

I know you have, you know, "fears" about getting involved with people. That you have a hard time trusting men. I mean, we've talked about this ad nauseam, every time you break up with someone. And I totally respect that because I've seen a lot of the clowns you've dated [and it's…]

JESS. [Whoa, who,] whoa!

MATT. I care about you and I'm telling you now: you pick really bad guys.

JESS. Say it louder. Did everyone catch that?

MATT. Everyone already knows that.

(She steps across the aisle to the glass case and points to one of the fully realized Dire Wolf models.)

JESS. You see this full-sized wolf model with all the teeth? I want you to put your face through this glass. And into that wolf's mouth.

MATT. Look, just, when I woke up...in the middle of a museum is where I have to, fine, okay, when I woke up? I thought, "Oh fuck, what if this wrecks our friendship?" But that's so fucking clichéd and I think it's totally worth the risk.

JESS. I bet I can change [your mind.]

MATT. [Because last] night was fantastic. I've never connected [like that before.]

JESS. [Please, Matt.] We really don't [need to...]

MATT. [So yes I do know] you and I know you're afraid but you [shouldn't...]

JESS. [I'm not] afraid!

(Pause. She moves closer to him, tries to tone the conversation down.)

Look, I didn't want to do this. You're great and I do love you, that is one hundred percent true, so I didn't want to have to, fuck, listen...last night was not good.

MATT. No, I understand why [you might...]

JESS. [No, no, the] sex. The sex was not good.

*(**MATT** suddenly seems to become aware of other people in the museum. **JESS** looks embarrassed. He laughs it off...)*

MATT. Shut the fuck up.

JESS. No, you picked this place and now, so you need to know. It was really bad, Matt. I'm sorry, okay, I don't know if it's better with other girls, it has to be, doesn't it? But with me it was really, just...bad.

MATT. What?

JESS. So I think it's better if [we just...]

MATT. [Bad?"]

JESS. If we just keep our friendship as is.

MATT. What does that mean, "bad?"

JESS. I don't know, it's hard to be specific.

MATT. Hard? Make it unhard. Less hard. Whatever.

JESS. Okay, it's not hard to be specific, I just don't want to be specific because people are really obviously listening.

MATT. I don't care.

JESS. Fine. You said you watched the movie here? About how they dig up the fossils?

MATT. I'm not letting you change the subject.

JESS. I'm not.

MATT. You're talking about fossils.

JESS. Just fucking, ugh, did you watch the movie?

MATT. I watched it.

JESS. The part about how back in the 1920s they used to use kerosene to clean the fossils. They would pour boiling kerosene on skulls like these to clean them.

MATT. So?

JESS. Matt.

MATT. Jess.

JESS. That's what the sex was like.

MATT. Okay. Okay. Okay, that was specific.

(It is awkward. Then quietly…)

I thought it was amazing.

JESS. I…know you did.

MATT. You seemed to really, I mean I thought we both…?

JESS. I didn't want to hurt your feelings.

MATT. So you were faking that?

JESS. Like you said, I've been with a lot of bad guys.

(Pause.)

MATT. I'm gonna go.

JESS. Oh, don't go.

MATT. Boiling oil.

JESS. It'll all be fine if we just don't talk about it.

MATT. Everything stripped to the bone, that's what it was like for you?

JESS. Maybe that was extreme. You backed me into a corner and it was fresh in my mind. But! But if we just pretend it didn't happen…?

MATT. I'm not gonna do that.

JESS. Well, I'm gonna go ahead and do that because it's better in the long run.

> *(She smiles apologetically and tries to take his hand. He pulls away.)*

MATT. No, I mean, I don't think I could do that if I wanted to at this point, but I don't want to pretend it didn't happen. And don't look at me like that, like I spilled something on your parent's couch and you're gonna cover for me.

JESS. I'm not.

MATT. You are.

JESS. Well you did spill on their couch and I did take the wrap because you're my friend and that's what friends do.

MATT. That was, like, five years ago and this isn't that kind of moment.

JESS. Clearly I'm floundering, I don't want to fuck up our friendship.

MATT. You didn't.

JESS. It feels like I did.

MATT. Well…

> *(He starts to leave.)*

JESS. Matt.

MATT. I'll talk to you later or something.

JESS. Matty.

MATT. Bye.

(He keeps going. **JESS** *mutters to herself, building up the courage…)*

JESS. Fuck. Fuck, fuck… Matt! God damn it. It was amazing, okay? It was amazing! I'm shouting in a museum, oh god, this is so, it was amazing!

*(***MATT*** *stops. She takes a breath and then…)*

Fine, fine, okay, fine, it was too amazing and I'm not saying that to make you feel, however, whatever, it was amazing and I wasn't ready for that and I don't know what to do with that and you were sleeping there and you looked so fucking adorable so I tried to run away, to a museum, to a fucking museum, because who would follow someone to a museum? You would, of course. And did! You tracked me down and bared your soul in front of a bunch of wolf skulls that are backlit orange for some awful reason that just makes everything here seem more intense anyway, doesn't it make everything seem more vivid somehow? I can't handle it, I could barely handle it before you started professing all this shit, and now I'm scared and I know you're right, which really pisses me off because you shouldn't know me better than I do, so it's like I don't know what to do but I didn't…

(He rushes back cutting her off with a kiss. Fireworks. They both smile.)

MATT. The security guards are going to throw you out of here for making a scene like that in front of extinct animals. You're disturbing the skulls. I mean, they're never gonna let you come back here.

JESS. Shut-up.

(More kissing. They break again.)

MATT. Seriously. Fuck you so much for that kerosene thing.

End of Play

Giant Robot
Love Story

GIANT ROBOT LOVE STORY was commissioned and produced by Gates McFadden. It premiered at The Actor's Gang as a part of *Krusher Does Krusher* on February 11, 2015. The production was directed by Gates McFadden. The cast was as follows:

DANNY . . . . Jonathan Del Arco
MATEO . . . . Gary Patent
DR. KRUSHER . . . . Gates McFadden

CHARACTERS

DANNY – a gay man

MATEO – a gay man

DR. KRUSHER – a woman, an iconic science fiction character

AUTHOR'S NOTES

[ ] = overlapping text

The roars in the script are canned sound and should be extremely loud.

At one point, the **COMPUTER** has a line. It should probably just be pre-recorded.

(DANNY and MATEO are both really good looking guys in their twenties or thirties. DANNY is trying to leave and he might even have a helmet of some kind. MATEO is pissed off and using a lot of "air quotes." DANNY keeps looking over his shoulder into the distance. There is urgency. Things are moving quickly.)

DANNY. I'm sorry, Mateo, I have [to go.]

MATEO. [I'm not done] with this [argument.]

DANNY. [I know, but] this is really, really important and I [can't just...]

MATEO. [See, there's] always "something else" you're running off to do.

(A roar from off stage. It's kind of awful. They both wince.)

DANNY. Listen, I have to go pilot this giant robot now. I have to go pilot this giant robot because I'm the only one standing between our survival and the total destruction of the city.

MATEO. Oh, okay, Danny, so you're "important" and I'm not?

DANNY. I really think piloting a giant robot to save many many thousands of lives merits a rain check on this discussion.

MATEO. It's not a "discussion," I'm pissed off because you never pay attention to me. Maybe that sounds selfish right now, right in this very moment, but I don't care. You never choose me, Danny. And you know damn well that someone else could totally pilot that giant robot.

DANNY. Actually, the robot is specifically calibrated to my brain and only my brain, so that's [not true.]

MATEO. [You're being] really "dramatic," right?

*(A roar from off stage; maybe even more awful.
They both wince.)*

DANNY. Mateo, I don't have time [for this.]

MATEO. [I mean, who] cares if the city gets destroyed? They tear down old buildings and replace them with newer, more "modern" buildings all the time. And the new buildings look better so this giant monster attack is just speeding up the inevitable.

DANNY. You're, wait, are you serious?

MATEO. Let the monster do the work.

DANNY. Okay, you're kind of a horrible person.

MATEO. Take that back!

DANNY. And you're a total science fiction junky. You love anything space or robot related, so don't pretend for one second my piloting that giant robot doesn't get you off. You should be rock hard right now.

MATEO. Stop talking about my private fantasies in public. And I'm not the one walking out on this relationship, Daniel Greg Winters.

DANNY. Walking out on the, shut up. Shut up. And don't use my full name. Look, I'm only going to be gone long enough to fight the enormous monster that's terrorizing the city and hopefully win! And then, assuming I'm not crippled or too psychologically fucked up, I'll come back and we can have brunch just like we planned.

MATEO. Mm hm, yep, and what happens if you don't win?

DANNY. Then I'll be dead!

MATEO. And how do you think that's going to make me feel?

(The monster roar is awful and deafening.)

DANNY. I can't with this right now, I [really can't.]

MATEO. [Abandoned. Alone.] Betrayed. Hurt. Unresolved. And I'll always have a horrible, burning vendetta to seek revenge against that giant monster for killing you.

DANNY. Well, at least that last part is kind of sweet.

MATEO. You want me to have to carry around a "horrible, burning vendetta?!"

DANNY. Mateo, I just, I don't know, I think you might be sort of psychotic.

MATEO. I will not feel guilty for standing up for "us."

DANNY. If the monster destroys the city and kills everyone, there won't be any "us" anymore!

MATEO. You always turn things around like that. I was talking to Keith about it and he totally agrees [with me.]

DANNY. [Perfect,] Keith, ya know, perfect.

MATEO. You don't like Keith?

DANNY. No, I don't. Here's why: Keith just wants to have sex with you and will therefore agree with anything you say. And that's annoying.

MATEO. At least Keith listens to me.

DANNY. Please stop talking to Keith about our personal life. And stop trying to pretend this is all a surprise to you or somehow unfair. This is who I am, Mateo, and it's who I've always been. I'm standing in front of you as the giant robot pilot you fetishized and fell in love with.

MATEO. When we started dating, [I didn't…]

DANNY. [When we started] dating, I was super up front about my job fighting unspeakable, awful monsters to keep the city safe. You knew what you were getting into. And it made you hot.

MATEO. But it's different [now and…]

DANNY. [Ah, ah, ah,] you knew. Look, I don't have time for this back and forth. If you won't listen to me, then listen to cult sci-fi icon Dr. Krusher!

> *(He motions to the side of the stage.* **DR. KRUSHER** *enters in uniform and potentially a lab coat. She means business.)*

MATEO. Holy shit!

DR. KRUSHER. Hello, Mateo. I hear you're a fan? Danny's told me a lot about you. Also, you are very handsome. I'm saying that to get on your good side, is it working? Danny said you were easily swayed by flattery.

MATEO. What?!

DANNY. Oh, come on.

DR. KRUSHER. Don't be mad, Mateo. Context is important. And did I mention that your eyes are beautiful?

MATEO. Stop that! What do you even have to do with "giant robots?" This isn't outer space; it's not even space themed. What does she have to do with "giant robots?"

DR. KRUSHER. Oh, air quotes? That's not at all "condescending."

DANNY. The giant monsters might be from outer space; it's a loose correlative. Listen, you're a fan of her show so just fucking go with it.

DR. KRUSHER. Mateo, I know I'm not Astro Boy, and trust me that I hate myself for not being Astro Boy, but I'm here to help. Now I don't want to speak for Danny, but I will. I suspect he thought, in the absence of an anime character somehow appearing in real life, this was the closest thing genre-wise he'd get to a science fiction icon that you might somehow identify with: sort of maternal and authoritative but still sexy in that way gay men find strong women sexy? It's a stretch but I'm game for the challenge. I had to dress up like an antiquated naval officer once. And I did it! Of course, this could all just be a holodeck simulation we're trapped in until the right sequence of events opens the doors. You'd be amazed how often that happens. People die, Mateo. People die in the holodecks all the time and then I have to pronounce them dead. They don't show that part, but I have to say, "They're dead."

MATEO. What's a holodeck?

DR. KRUSHER. It's a simulated reality facility located on starships and star bases. Mateo, I'm embarrassed for you. Danny, I thought you said he was a fan? This only works if he's a fan.

(The monster roars!)

DANNY. He is a fan! We both are. We're just always stoned when we watch it on YouTube. Medicinally stoned.

DR. KRUSHER. Huh. No residuals from YouTube, just so you know.

DANNY. Dr Krusher, I'm so sorry but can we get on with it? I don't mean to rush you and I'm super grateful, but I really do [need to go.]

DR. KRUSHER. [Yes, of course.] This would just be a lot easier if he had a firmer grasp on the basic underpinnings of the series.

MATEO. Hey!

DR. KRUSHER. Oh, Mateo, I'm not trying to belittle you. I don't need to do that, you're already little. And you're also a really poor excuse for a fan boy, so I'll dispense with the references and cut to the chase. You're making this civil disaster about you.

MATEO. It's important to have communication in a relationship.

DR. KRUSHER. No, it's not. And your timing is terrible and selfish. Also, you're displaying a quality that has ruined so many men; you're being, oh, what's the word? Computer, what is the word I'm looking for?

COMPUTER. "Needy."

> (**MATEO** *and* **DANNY** *both look around, startled by the voice.*)

MATEO. Where the fuck did that come from?

DR. KRUSHER. The computer.

MATEO. What computer?!

DR. KRUSHER. Now Mateo, look at Danny. He is the hero of this story. You're technically the protagonist, but he's the hero. And he clearly loves you in spite of your many, many faults. And they are glaring. In fact, I'm guessing you must be an incredible bottom for him to put up with all this; I mean the fuck of the century. Am I right? I'm not even flattering you now, that just must be true. Anyway, Danny has a job to do and you need to let him go do it with your emotional support and love.

>   *(Pause.)*

MATEO. Fine.

>   **(DANNY** *kisses* **MATEO**. *The loudest of all roars sounds. Everything shakes from the proximity and volume.)*

DANNY. Now I'll go save the city.

>   *(He rushes off. Leaving* **DR. KRUSHER** *and* **MATEO**.*)*

MATEO. If you survive, we're totally breaking up!!

DR. KRUSHER. Mateo, even though this is all ostensibly taking place at some point in the future, I'm going to prescribe you some good old-fashioned Xanax.

End of Play

Aquarium

AQUARIUM was commissioned and produced by Dad's Garage Theatre Company (Kate Warner, Artistic Director; Kathryn Colegrove, Managing Director) and premiered on November 4, 2005 in the Top Shelf Theatre as a part of the short play cycle *Sleepy*. The production was directed by Kate Warner. The cast was as follows:

MAY . . . . .Alison Hastings

STRANGER . . . . Wade Tilton

CHARACTERS

MAY – a young woman, a self-styled hero, her perspective on the world
is skewed entirely by a single horrific event in her childhood

STRANGER – an seemingly warm and sincere man who is either sparing
May's feelings or a sociopath

AUTHOR'S NOTES

[ ] indicate overlapping dialogue.

The projections should be as large and consuming as possible.

(A small hotel room: bed, side table, lamp, and an older model phone with a coiled cord. It's an insanely long cord. The kind of thing that's easy to get tangled up in.)

(MAY enters, flustered and breathing heavy, crashing onto the bed. After a moment, she rolls over, turns on the lamp and picks up the phone. Before she can dial, she notices her wet shoes. She puts the phone receiver back, removes them, and looks at them with disappointment. Her attention returns to the phone.)

(She picks it up, hesitates, and then dials. She waits.)

MAY. Hello? Hi. Hi. It's me. It's May. May. May. I know, hi. Okay, I need to…

I'm in a hotel, some kitschy vintage hotel, but the room is little. Very small. Or it feels small. And there's a lamp that isn't bright enough to make sense as a lamp. I'm getting distracted. Look, I did it again tonight, right at closing. I shattered the jellyfish tank. Again. But I was almost caught by the security guards. Like this aquarium was a much bigger, like a much larger affair across the board. A lot nicer, more funding I guess, definitely thicker glass, I mean I had to hit it over and over again until it broke. But I got away.

I did leave the lead pipe though. So that's not great. So maybe they'll find me this time. Fingerprints or something, but I got away for now. Oh, and they maybe had cameras. My shoes got ruined again. Look, I want to tell you, in case they catch me, I want to tell you some things.

(She holds the phone away from her ear as if avoiding yelling.)

I'm telling you why! Stop yelling!

Okay, so these are the important things. I love the jellyfish. I've loved them ever since I was a little girl. I don't want them to die. I'm not trying to hurt them. That's important. I just want them to not be in glass boxes, on display. Trapped. Trapped. Can you imagine what that feels like?

Like I had a little fish bowl once and I always felt bad for the fish. Like we were both stuck, the fish in the bowl, me in my room, in my bed. In the dark. My bedroom was down a long hall from my parents' room. I'm sure it wasn't especially long for a hallway, but to me it seemed very, very far. And after they tucked me in, I wouldn't hear a sound until the next morning. The only sound was the chain on the ceiling fan in my room knocking against the light. Because of the spinning. Tap. Tap. Tap. Tap. Tap. Tap.

But I liked that sound, it was constant and kind of... Tap. Tap. Soothing. And I would watch that fish, just swimming. Swimming around. And even though I thought it maybe wasn't fair, I still liked having my fish.

Then one night, this is important, too, only one time, one night, I heard a noise. It startled me, scared me, because it wasn't a noise I had ever heard before and it was so different from the ceiling fan. I snuck out of bed and made my way down the hall. My parents' bedroom door was cracked open. They usually kept it closed, all the way closed, but it was open just a little. So I pushed it a little bit more and took one step in...

(Lights rise to reveal a man seated in a chair just out of the light. He is in a shirt and tie with slacks. His sleeves are rolled up and his hands are clearly wet with something. He's holding a knife. His face is obscured by shadow.)

There was a table and chair across the room from my
parents' bed. The way the lamp sat on the table, I could
only see him from the neck down, and he just sat there.
But I could feel him looking at me. The light coming in
from the windows was very dim and I could kind of see
my parents in bed. Or I could see that they were in bed.
I mostly remember the man's hands. He was holding
something...

STRANGER. Hello there.

> *(The sound of a film projector slowly cranks into*
> *effect as images of schools of jellyfish are projected*
> *onto the wall behind her. When* **MAY** *moves, she*
> *pulls the receiver with her, tangling up in the cord.)*

MAY. And he started talking to me. I think I should have
been afraid, I was afraid, but I was still half asleep and
none of it seemed very real to me. And I was curious.

STRANGER. Hello there.

MAY. Hello?

STRANGER. Did we wake you? I'm sorry. We didn't mean to
wake you up.

MAY. That's okay.

STRANGER. Well, all right.

MAY. What are you doing?

STRANGER. Your Mommy and Daddy and I are working on
something.

MAY. Okay.

STRANGER. Let me see how to explain it. Hmmm...

MAY. I'm pretty smart.

STRANGER. I'm sure you are. Okay, what did you do today?
Did you do something with your parents, anything
special?

MAY. We went to the zoo.

STRANGER. Really? Do you like the zoo?

MAY. No.

STRANGER. No?

MAY. I don't like the cages. I don't like the bars. Oh, but I like the aquarium. Because that's glass so it's different. I like it there a lot.

STRANGER. I know, your parents told me. Can you believe that? And what's your favorite part of the aquarium? When you go, what is your favorite thing?

MAY. The jellyfish.

STRANGER. Oh, jellyfish, those are my favorite too. I could watch them for hours.

MAY. Mmm hmm.

STRANGER. They're almost magical aren't they?

MAY. Yes. They're lovely.

STRANGER. They are. And so are you. And you're a very special little girl, too. You'll never guess, but your parents wanted to surprise you with something special. We were planning something special. And I'm here to help.

MAY. What kind of surprise?

STRANGER. Well I shouldn't tell you. I would [ruin the…]

MAY. [Please?]

STRANGER. I don't [know…?]

MAY. [Please!]

STRANGER. Okay, but it's a secret, just between us. Your parents wanted to do something very special for you, because they love you so much, and they know how you love jellyfish. So as a special treat they're, and this is how very much they love you, they're turning into jellyfish. Just for you.

MAY. Just for me!

STRANGER. Just for you.

MAY. How?

STRANGER. Well I can't tell you, but we've been working on it all night. And we've still got a ways to go. But you'll be so happy in the end.

MAY. Can I see them now?

STRANGER. Oh no, I'm sorry honey. It wouldn't be good for you to turn the lights on; they're not ready for you yet. But it's okay if you want to give them a really quick hug. Do you want to give them a hug [before you...]

MAY. [But jellyfish] will sting you. Mommy always says that.

STRANGER. Just a quick hug, they won't sting you. I promise. They love you.

MAY. My eyes were starting to adjust a little, I still couldn't see his face, but I could make out the bed and see my parents a little. I walked over and realized that they were making these very quiet noises. Little noises. And moving the tiniest bit, like breathing but very shallow, very sharp. I reached my arms out to hug my Daddy and when I touched him, he jerked. His body was wet and parts of it felt warm and parts of him moved when I touched him. I stopped because he was shaking so hard.

STRANGER. Maybe that's enough.

> (*The* STRANGER *rises from his chair.*)

MAY. And it was enough. It was enough, because they weren't jellyfish, they weren't, how could I not, like a stupid little girl, they were lying there, trying to, all they could do was lie there while I talked to this man, this man in their room, they were helpless.

> (*She tries to step away, but is tangled in the phone cord. She drops the receiver and rips the phone free. She grabs the* STRANGER'*s chair and smashes it into the wall where the images of jellyfish are playing...*)

All I did was fucking stand there! And believe that some man, some stranger, some magical stranger was turning them into jellyfish!!

> (*She drops the chair and sinks to the floor. The jellyfish image fades from the back wall of the hotel room.*)

STRANGER. Come along now.

MAY. I didn't know.

STRANGER. Come along, you must be so sleepy.

MAY. Yes, sleepy. Okay. Goodnight. I love you, Mommy and Daddy. I promise to take care of you when you're jellyfish. I'll take care of you and I promise I'll never let anyone put you in a tank. Ever. What a lovely surprise.

STRANGER. Very special.

MAY. Yes.

STRANGER. Let's get you back into bed.

>   *(The **STRANGER** sets his knife on the table and rises...)*

MAY. And I took his hand. I took his...

STRANGER. All right?

MAY. He didn't seem to mind that my hands were wet from my parents. His hands were too. We walked down the hall, that long hallway. He tucked me into bed and...

>   *(She notices the phone receiver on the floor and picks it up.)*

He tucked me into bed and...

STRANGER. It's all right.

MAY. And I went to sleep. Like nothing, like I hadn't even been awake. But in the morning, the next morning, I woke up and I was so excited. I jumped out of bed and bolted down that hall, which suddenly seemed so much shorter, throwing the door open to my parents room.

STRANGER. [Everything's all right.]

MAY. [They were gone: my] parents, the man, the sheets and blankets, just a bare mattress and nothing. Disappeared. No jellyfish. And I was filled with this, this rage. I thought he took them. He took them somewhere. Liar. I remember I thought he would put them in a tank, behind glass, keep them somewhere and I promised. I promised I would never let that happen, behind glass, on display, trapped. And now I can't help myself. I don't know, it's ridiculous, I don't know. But it's better if they're jellyfish, it's better to believe that. Than to believe what he may have been doing to them. But if they're jellyfish, just like all the other jellyfish, how can I tell which ones are my parents.

STRANGER. [Everything's all right.]

MAY. [How can I tell which] ones or where he took them? Which ones they even are? I can't. That's right. That's right.

That's why I have to free all of them.

(The light on the **STRANGER** *fades out.)*

Hello? Hello, hi, are you still there? I hope I didn't scare you. You can talk now if you want. Hello?

(She looks at the phone and gently puts it back on the receiver.)

End of Play

Serendipity

SERENDIPITY was commissioned and produced by City Theatre in Miami, Florida as a part of *Summer Shorts 18* (John Manzelli, Producing Artistic Director and Susan Westfall, Literary Director) and premiered at the Adrienne Arsht Center for the Performing Arts on June 6, 2013. The production was directed by Margaret Ledford. The cast was as follows:

MAN	Ken Clement
WOMAN	Renata Eastlick
PASSERBY 1	Irene Adjan
PASSERBY 2	Todd Allen Durkin
PASSERBY 3	Rayner Garranchan
PASSERBY 4	Vera Varlamov

CHARACTERS

MAN – a man, sort of an everyman, but grumpy
WOMAN – a woman, could be nicer, a bit "high end"
PASSERBY 1 – a woman, naïve, polite, but less "high end"
PASSERBY 2 – a man, probably a recreational drug user
PASSERBY 3 – a man, Passerby 4's husband
PASSERBY 4 – a woman, Passerby 3's wife

AUTHOR'S NOTES

[ ] and [[ ]] in the script indicate overlapping dialogue.

The play wants to tumble ahead swiftly and at a pace with no stops and no time to clarify. So let it do that.

*(A **MAN** is standing on a street corner. He wears a hat. He is intently watching something across the street.)*

MAN. So I was just standing there on the street, late at night. I had hoped to grab an early edition of the paper, but all the machines were still empty. That's been my luck lately, like I'm never in the right place at the right time. Anyway, I caught him out of the corner of my eye, the way something grabs your attention a little, enough to make you stop. I looked across the street and, over in front of the new hotel, a man was kissing a woman. They were under a streetlight alone together, kind of like a postcard. An old postcard, before everything became so ironic. I looked for just a minute, and then I started to move along when suddenly they broke apart and I saw him, the man kissing the woman across the street in front of the new hotel. I mean I saw his face. Not just his face: his build, his coat, his hat. He looked exactly like me. I don't mean he was similar to me, I mean, and this is weird right, but he looked exactly like me. It was unreal, surreal, I don't know. Suddenly a cab pulled up and he hopped in, all very quick, saying goodbye to the woman and away and vanished. He was gone before I could even move, so I tried to catch up with the woman.

WOMAN. I was standing on the street, right in front of that new hotel. It's so garish, all modern and "sleek." Ugh. But my boyfriend really, no, no, my fiancé, sorry.

(She flashes an engagement ring.)

Maybe not the best ring shopper. But he loves restaurants, so we had dinner there. Again. Third time in two weeks. In fact, he had just left in a cab when this strange man came towards me. Very strange, not threatening or anything, just, well, just strange.

MAN. Excuse me. Excuse me, [ma'am.]

WOMAN. [I'm sorry,] I don't have any money.

MAN. No, I don't need [any money...]

WOMAN. [I make a point] of not giving money to strangers on the street.

MAN. No, no I'm not, who was that man? That just left in the cab?

WOMAN. Oh, that was my boyfriend Mark. Fiancé actually, we just got engaged. I forget sometimes, it's so new. Mark Sanders, do you know him?

MAN. No, no, I thought I did, but it's just that [he looked...]

WOMAN. [Listen, I] really need to get going.

MAN. He looked exactly like me.

WOMAN. What?

MAN. Your boyfriend looked exactly like me.

WOMAN. I'm sorry, but are you just crazy?

MAN. It was very shocking. I saw you two from across the street and he could have been my twin.

WOMAN. Oh, but you don't look anything like him. Mark is very attractive.

MAN. Okay, at this point the woman got a little insulting. It was almost like she was implying that I wasn't attractive.

WOMAN. I wasn't trying to be mean, but this guy looked nothing like Mark at all. It was just bizarre. And I felt very uncomfortable. Oh and then, to make matters worse, this woman with a quaint hairstyle and a knock-off handbag walked up to us...

PASSERBY 1. I was walking down the street in front of that fancy new hotel. It looks nice, but I hear the rooms are really small. Boutique or whatever the fancy term for overpriced is right now.

WOMAN. I mean it was just a really obvious knock-off handbag.

PASSERBY 1. Anyway, I saw my friends Jim and Sally in front of the restaurant. It looked like maybe they were fighting, so I almost passed by, but then I thought that would be rude if they happened to notice me "sneaking" by, so I decided to stop and say hello...

MAN. So I'm trying to talk to this kind of insulting woman when some other strange woman walks up with a big smile.

PASSERBY 1. Jim, Sally, hey you two! I hope I'm not interrupting. I was going to slip by, but this is just so serendipitous, running into you, isn't it?

MAN. My name's not Jim.

WOMAN. I'm sorry, who are you?

PASSERBY 1. Come on you guys; don't be silly.

WOMAN. Do you two know each other? Is this some kind of weird thing that you do to people on the street?

MAN. What?

WOMAN. Because I won't be a part of it and I've already said very clearly that I'm not giving you any money.

MAN. I've never met this woman before in my life. Seriously, I'm just trying to find out more about your boyfriend.

WOMAN. Fiancé.

(She brandishes the ring aggressively.)

Got it? And you look nothing like him. Isn't it possible that you simply made a mistake? You were standing way over there for [Christ's sake.]

PASSERBY 1. [You two are] acting very strange. Sally, are [you feeling...?]

WOMAN. [My name] is not Sally. This is ridiculous; I'm leaving.

(She begins to walk away. MAN *and* PASSERBY 1 *move with her...)*

MAN. Oh no, not until I get some [answers.]

PASSERBY 1. [Jim, what] is wrong [with her?]

MAN. [I'm not] Jim. Can you give us a minute?

WOMAN. Listen, we don't need a minute. You look about as much like Mark as her bag looks like real Prada.

PASSERBY 1. What's wrong with my bag?

MAN. Just stop for two seconds please!

PASSERBY 2. I was standing on the corner across the street from that new hotel. I was waiting for the walk signal that was taking forever. Sometimes when it's later at night it feels like the lights never change, ya now? So I'm standing there just staring at it thinking: change, change, change, change. Like that's gonna' do any good, right? But wait, all right, ya never know, superstitions and how your brain works, like crossing railroad tracks, cemeteries and holding your breath, or that dream where you're falling and wake up right before you hit the ground and you're breathing all crazy and, just, heady stuff like that, so I'm looking at the light I'm thinking: change, change, change, and maybe it will. But then I see these people crossing against the light, which is, just, dangerous.

PASSERBY 1. Right when [we got to the other side...]

MAN. [That stupid woman [[wouldn't] stop following us...]]

WOMAN. [[I couldn't shake these two crazies and...]]

PASSERBY 2. Hey! You people should pay more attention. You didn't even look to see if any cars were coming and if a car actually hits you then it's [not gonna...]

WOMAN. [There aren't] even any cars around?

PASSERBY 2. You didn't even look. Just walked out into the... Susan, is that you?

WOMAN. Oh for the love [of God.]

PASSERBY 1. [No, this] is Sally and her husband Jim.

WOMAN. Would you please just stop!

MAN. I am not Jim, and I don't know you or her. I'm trying to figure out why I look just like her boyfriend [Mark.]

WOMAN. [Fiancé!]

> *(She holds her hand up and, with exaggeration, points to the ring.)*

MAN. Her fiancé [Mark.]

PASSERBY 1. I could have just walked by, you know? I didn't have to be polite.

(**MAN** *and* **WOMAN** *glare at her.*)

PASSERBY 2. Sorry; it's the light I guess. Or something. You look a lot like my little sister's college roommate Susan. Susan Jenkins? Do you know her?

WOMAN. No. No, I do not know her.

MAN. Are you serious?

PASSERBY 1. Wait, I know a Susan Jenkins.

MAN. Oh, come on!

PASSERBY 1. Wow, this is so serendipitous.

WOMAN. Stop using that word; no one uses that word.

PASSERBY 1. I don't know what I was thinking; you don't look like Sally at all. But you do strongly resemble Susan.

PASSERBY 2. But I think Susan's kind of shorter.

PASSERBY 1. Sure.

PASSERBY 2. And Susan doesn't ever wear those crazy high heels.

WOMAN. Watch it.

PASSERBY 1. And is maybe a bit less concerned with appearances.

WOMAN. So this lady was clearly looking for a fight. It's bad enough to be chased down the street by a pack of insane people. But for this woman of questionable fashion taste to be basically calling me shallow out in public? Well, that was about all I could take.

MAN. So these two people had just steam rolled their way into my conversation with nonsense about Jim and Sally and Susan were really getting on my nerves. It's amazing how some people can be so single-minded about things that it crosses the line into blatant rudeness. All I wanted was a few minutes to talk to this woman about her boyfriend who looked like me.

PASSERBY 1. It was foolish in hindsight to think those two people were Sally and Jim. I mean, it seems really unlikely that Sally and Jim would even be at that hotel. They are not fans of eating out and they live all the way across town. Also, Sally loves my bag.

PASSERBY 2. Susan is just crazy beautiful. I was really only being nice after that first mix-up.

PASSERBY 1. Sally's commented on how much she likes my bag before, many times, on the craftsmanship.

PASSERBY 2. Because, between us, there's honestly not much of a resemblance.

(PASSERSBY 3 & 4 enter.)

PASSERBY 3. I was standing just down the block from that new hotel.

PASSERBY 4. We were standing.

PASSERBY 3. We. Yes. We were heading home from the market that's open late.

PASSERBY 4. The only one that's open late.

PASSERBY 3. Well, it wasn't my idea to move to this neighborhood.

PASSERBY 4. Really? Right now is when you want to talk about this?

PASSERBY 3. Anyway, I don't know why I looked up at that hotel, but something caught my eye, kinda' grabbed my attention.

PASSERBY 4. He just stopped, in the middle of the street. My first thought was "Why does everything with this man have to be so difficult?" But then I saw it, too.

(They stop and look up.)

WOMAN. Look, this has been sufficiently odd. Good night.

(The group begins moving with her again.)

MAN. Wait, [I'm sorry, can you, I mean I haven't got to speak with you yet...]

PASSERBY 1. [Look I'm really [[sorry about this. I haven't been sleeping lately...]]]

PASSERBY 2. [[So it wasn't very cool to snap at you guys about the traffic light…]]

> (*They bump into* **PASSERSBY 3 & 4** *who are both looking up.*)

PASSERBY 3. Hey, watch where [you're going.]

PASSERBY 4. [You see us] standing here.

MAN. You [watch out.]

PASSERBY 2. [Why are you] standing right in the middle of the street?

PASSERSBY 3 & 4. Look.

WOMAN. What? It's an ugly hotel.

PASSERBY 1. Oh, you think it's ugly?

WOMAN. Well, I mean it's fine if you like that whole modern thing.

PASSERBY 1. I wonder about the color.

WOMAN. The color is awful.

PASSERBY 1. And I hear the rooms are almost claustrophobic, and at those prices.

PASSERSBY 3 & 4. No, up on the ledge.

> (**PASSERSBY 3 & 4** *both point more specifically. The group gasps.*)

WOMAN. Oh no.

PASSERBY 2. What is that guy doing [up there?]

MAN. [We should let] the hotel management [know.]

PASSERSBY 3 & 4. [We should] call the police.

PASSERBY 2. Whoa, that's [bizarre.]

PASSERBY 1. [It doesn't] look [safe.]

PASSERBY 2. [Whoa,] whoa, seriously, that guy looks just like you.

> (*All of the people squint up at the ledge and then turn to look at the* **MAN** *next to them, eyes widening.*)

PASSERSBY 3 & 4. Spooky.

MAN. No look…

(The **MAN** *takes off his hat.)*

See, that's someone else all together.

WOMAN. He looks exactly like you.

MAN. No, he [doesn't, he…]

WOMAN. [He looks] exactly like you!

(He pauses, gazing up at the **MAN.** *Then with recognition…)*

MAN. Oh my God.

(All of the people return their attention to the roof.)

I had to admit that the man on the roof looked like me; even more so maybe than the man in the cab. In a disquieting way, in a way that made me not want to look. And I thought what are the odds? What are the odds of two other men looking exactly like me?

WOMAN. Do you have a brother or something?

PASSERBY 2. He's even in the same clothes. What are the odds?

PASSERBY 3. He could even be you.

PASSERBY 4. He could, he could absolutely be you.

PASSERBY 1. What would you even be doing up there?

MAN. Don't ask me.

PASSERBY 1. It's so serendipitous.

WOMAN. All right, look, you clearly have no idea what that word actually means, nothing about this situation is fortunate or in any way…

(The **WOMAN** *is suddenly struck by a thought and inhales sharply.)*

PASSERBY 1. What is it?

WOMAN. What if he, what if you jump?

PASSERBY 2. You wouldn't do that, [would you?]

PASSERBY 1. [You never] know about people.

MAN. Of course I wouldn't jump.

WOMAN. Then what in the hell are you doing up there?

MAN. I don't know!

PASSERBY 2. That fall will kill you.

PASSERBY 3. Instantly, your heart might even stop on the way down.

PASSERBY 4. I think that's just a myth.

PASSERBY 1. No, I think that actually happens: your heart just stops.

PASSERSBY 3 & 4. You better not jump.

MAN. I won't.

PASSERBY 1. They're right; it would kill you [for sure.]

MAN. [I'm not] gonna' jump!

WOMAN. Really, you look like Mark, okay? Does that make you happy? I'll tell you whatever you want if you come down off the roof.

PASSERBY 1. You're sort of rewarding his behavior.

PASSERSBY 3 & 4. It is a cry for attention.

PASSERBY 1. Absolutely.

PASSERBY 2. So then, like, he'll totally climb up there and do this all again the next time he doesn't get what he wants.

WOMAN. Well I don't want him to jump do I?

MAN. Hello, I'm standing right here.

WOMAN. Of course, of course you are. So stay with us down here and come down off the roof.

MAN. This group of people had gone completely insane as far as I was concerned. That was not me. I didn't think it's me anyway, and I certainly wouldn't jump, for any reason I know.

PASSERBY 1. What is wrong with your fiancé?

WOMAN. He's not my, I don't even know him! He's just some stranger who tried to talk to me on the street and then climbed out on a ledge, it's not my fault.

(She turns back to the ledge.)

Listen up there, you stop this foolishness [right now!]

MAN. [I'm standing] right [here!]

PASSERBY 2. [See, see] that, he's just getting twitchier.

PASSERSBY 3 & 4. More agitated.

MAN. Stop it!

PASSERBY 1. Like a child.

WOMAN. I'll tell you that you look like anyone you want me to, but you come down off that ledge right now and stop frightening everyone!

MAN. Listen, you can all just cut it out. Even if that, and let me be really clear that I am in no way conceding this point, but even if that is me up on that ledge, I have absolutely no reason to jump. Every single day of my life is absolutely normal, nothing bad ever happens, nothing ever happens, nothing, in fact, this, this right now is the strangest thing that has ever happened in my life. And if that were me, then who am I? That would make me some other guy getting a cab and driving away, some other guy with another life and a fiancé and everything I don't have because I don't have anything or anything to do and none of you know me, no one knows me, I'm all alone. Alone. I don't even remember how I got here. But that doesn't matter, no, okay, no, because I think I know myself better than...

> (*They all lunge forward, holding their hands out, pointing in shock as the* **MAN** *jumps off the building...*)

WOMAN. [Oh my God!]

PASSERBY 1. [No, no, no!]

PASSERBY 2. [Whoa!]

PASSERSBY 3 & 4. [Oh no!]

> (*blackout*)

End of Play

Joshua Consumed
An Unfortunate Pear

JOSHUA CONSUMED AN UNFORTUNATE PEAR was commissioned and produced by City Theatre in Miami, Florida as a part of *Summer Shorts 19* (John Manzelli, Producing Artistic Director and Susan Westfall, Literary Director) and premiered at the Adrienne Arsht Center for the Performing Arts on June 12, 2014. The production was directed by John Manzelli. The cast was as follows:

JOSHUA . . . . Tom Wahl

AMELIA . . . . Nikki Fridh

DEATH . . . . .Elizabeth Dimon

CHORUS . . . . .Irene Adjan, David Perez-Ribada, Mcley Lafrance
Mary Sansone

CHARACTERS

JOSHUA – a man, sort of an everyman, a little too obsessed with the big things and definitely not the best at being attentive

AMELIA – a woman, Joshua's wife, frustrated by all of the little things, way past grand gestures, and filled with a rage she doesn't like

DEATH – a woman, busy, fond of making an entrance, annoyed when her precious time is wasted

CHORUS – a group of people with a lot of inside information, a knack for moving and speaking in unison, and a penchant for honesty regardless of the circumstances. Maybe they're all immortal like Joshua. Maybe they're all injured in weird ways. But they're still upbeat.

AUTHOR'S NOTES

When things get bloody, they should really get bloody. You could probably just put a bucket of the stuff under the small table and let it spray on the walls. Head wounds bleed a lot.

(**JOSHUA**, *a bit of an everyman but beat up,*
bruised, probably with a bloody gauze bandage
on his forehead and a black eye, sits in one of
two chairs at a small table. It has a floor length
tablecloth. The other chair is empty. He is eating a
green pear. It's juicy. A wooden bowl on the table
holds more pears.)

(*As he eats, a group of people enters. They move as*
a group. They speak as a group. They speak to the
audience. They are a **CHORUS**.)

CHORUS. This is Joshua eating a pear
　　Happy with his delicious choice
　　Trust us; it tastes like no other
　　This bite you see extends his life
　　Not just a bit but forever

　　This is Joshua eating a pear
　　And now he can't die, not ever
　　Trust us, even if you stabbed him
　　Over and over and over and over
　　And over again with a knife

JOSHUA. This pear is fantastic!

CHORUS. He really enjoys the pear.

JOSHUA. Ugh, you have no idea.

　　　　(**AMELIA** *enters in a form-fitting cardigan, a pencil*
　　　　skirt and heels. She carries a lightweight jacket and
　　　　wears a fashionable hat. She is beautiful. She also
　　　　carries on a small suitcase. She sets it down.)

AMELIA. Well, you look like you got your ass kicked. But I
　　see your big quest to find those "magical immortality
　　pears" was successful.

JOSHUA. They're so delicious.

AMELIA. They just look like pears. I'm unimpressed.

JOSHUA. You have to have one, Amelia.

CHORUS. This is Amelia.

    She doesn't want a pear.

AMELIA. No, thank you.

JOSHUA. Why are you wearing a hat?

CHORUS. This is Amelia.

    She enjoys a jaunty hat.

AMELIA. It's a bit windy outside.

JOSHUA. Are you going out?

AMELIA. I have a suitcase and I'm wearing a hat, Joshua. What do you think?

JOSHUA. I think that I fought many ferocious beasts to win these pears so we could live forever together in love and happiness. So you should cancel your plans, sit down, and eat some of this eternal life I won for us.

AMELIA. And who asked you to do that?

JOSHUA. Who asked me to get us eternal life?

AMELIA. I asked you to stop by the store and get some fresh milk. Did you do that? No, of course not. I asked you to do one little thing and instead you went on some big adventure, risked your life, and got us magical immortality pears, but look in the fridge and there's still no milk.

JOSHUA. I didn't realize getting the milk was such a big deal.

AMELIA. I know!

    (She grabs one of the pears and smashes it on the ground. She steps on the pear a few times, smashing it to further make her point.)

JOSHUA. Now you're just being wasteful.

AMELIA. Ha!

JOSHUA. So to be clear, you don't want to be immortal?

CHORUS. This is Amelia.

    She doesn't want to be immortal.

AMELIA. Be quiet.

JOSHUA. I kind of wish you'd told me you didn't want to be immortal before I went and risked my life so we could be together forever.

AMELIA. I kind of wish you were a more attentive partner, more engaged in our home life, and better in bed so I'd want to be together forever.

JOSHUA. Whoa.

AMELIA. Yep.

CHORUS. This is Amelia.

She's less than satisfied.

JOSHUA. Shut-up!

AMELIA. No, they're right. That is accurate. I am less than satisfied.

JOSHUA. This is sort of coming out of nowhere.

AMELIA. Oh my God, that's because you don't pay attention. Ever! Did I ever once express any interest in magical immortality pears? Did I? When you said you were going to find them, what did I say?

JOSHUA. You said, "It's too dangerous, don't go."

AMELIA. I said, "It's too dangerous, don't go."

JOSHUA. I thought you were expressing concern, heartfelt concern?!

AMELIA. I was expressing, "I'm not ready to break up yet so I'll feign concern in an effort to keep you from doing something crazy."

JOSHUA. Well, that's some bullshit.

AMELIA. It's called "communication."

CHORUS. Joshua is correct to call Amelia on her bullshit.

AMELIA. Huh. Okay, fine. Maybe it was less than honest, but it doesn't change the fact you're inattentive and a terrible lover.

JOSHUA. Fucking stop saying that; I always get you off.

CHORUS. Joshua is incorrect in stating that he always gets her off.

JOSHUA. Wait, what?

AMELIA. I hate our sex life.

JOSHUA. Our sex life is great!

AMELIA. Really?!

JOSHUA. I don't know, yes? But look, okay, I'm getting older and sometimes it's not as easy to perform. And sometimes I'm just tired. And, okay, sometimes maybe I rush it now; I'm willing to own that.

AMELIA. Do you know how I would describe our sex life? To other people? If other people asked? I'd say, "Oh, I suppose our sex life is like one of those old black and white movies where Godzilla destroys Tokyo."

JOSHUA. Oh, come on!

AMELIA. And I'm Tokyo!!

> *(She makes small Godzilla noises. And mimes tiny claws.)*

JOSHUA. Amelia.

> *(She makes larger Godzilla noises, scoops up some of the smashed pear from the floor, and throws it at him.)*

Calm down!

AMELIA. I'm calm!

CHORUS. This is Amelia
She's not really calm

AMELIA. No, no, I'm totally calm. I'm breathing. I'm breathing. I just get so mad. The sex thing is bad, but I don't want you to think that's why I'm leaving you. Sex goes downhill, that's a reality of long-term relationships that I'm fully prepared to accept. I suppose, if I have to. More importantly, you don't treat me well. I can't literally spend forever with a guy who's too self-involved to take care of me.

JOSHUA. Okay, here we go.

AMELIA. Not in a needy way. You just make me so angry. I'm filled with this rage!

JOSHUA. Look, every relationship has problems. That's why they're called relationships. People have to "relate" to one and other. It's an ongoing process. I'm sorry that you hate our sex life and I'm sorry you are feeling neglected. I am. But I just killed a bunch of monsters to get us immortality, so clearly 'm looking out for the relationship. Maybe, and I'm saying maybe, maybe you need to work on communicating your feelings and desires in a less passive aggressive way?

(It's clear he thinks he's being really understanding. **AMELIA***'s eyes go wide and she clenches her fists with rage.)*

CHORUS. This is Joshua
He started out on the right track
But then the train really derailed

JOSHUA. Wait, what did I say wrong?

AMELIA. Oh my God.

JOSHUA. No, I was just trying to explain things from my perspective.

AMELIA. Oh my God!!!

JOSHUA. I'm sorry!

AMELIA. Sorry for what?!

JOSHUA. I don't know!!

AMELIA. It's not your fault. Ugh. It is, but you can't help it. And I'm miserable!!

JOSHUA. Please, Amelia, I don't want you to be unhappy. I can make it better, I can change; I know I can change.

AMELIA. No, you can't!

JOSHUA. Yes, I can! Not by myself, but with your help. Tell me what to do.

(She picks up her suitcase and begins to leave.)

AMELIA. Goodbye.

JOSHUA. There has to be something I can do. I'm going to live forever now and I can't live forever without you. Yell at me if you're angry. Hit me. Beat me. Just don't leave. I'll do anything. Anything!

AMELIA. Anything?

JOSHUA. Yes! Yes.

CHORUS. This is Amelia
She has a flicker of an idea

AMELIA. You just make me irate. And I don't have anywhere to put that anger.

JOSHUA. I'm terrible. I'm the worst. Please forgive me. What can I do?

(She sets down her suitcase, opens it, and takes out a hammer.)

AMELIA. You ate one of those stupid magical immortality pears, right?

JOSHUA. Yes. Why? What are you gonna do with that hammer?

AMELIA. Nothing.

*(She rushes towards him with a scream and hits him in the head, sending him crashing behind the table. Breathing heavy, she waits. **DEATH** enters in a red suit, red heels, and a red scarf. She's ringing a hand bell. It should probably be a large hand bell. She stops when she sees **AMELIA**. She glances behind the table and makes a face.)*

DEATH. Did you strike him with that hammer?

*(**AMELIA** quickly hides the hammer behind her back and plays it cool.)*

AMELIA. I beg your pardon?

CHORUS. This is Amelia.
She struck him with a hammer.

*(**AMELIA** laughs nervously.)*

AMELIA. Just ignore them.

DEATH. What a mess. And I just had this pantsuit dry cleaned. It's dry clean only. Fancy, right? More like inconvenient. Well, I suppose I've seen worse messes. Oh, I'm death. The death. And I'm here to collect him. I ring the bell so people know I'm coming. Do you like it? It's so brassy. Makes for quite an entrance. Unfortunately, the sound can be confusing. Sometimes dead people think they're going to get ice cream, but they're not. Oh God damn it, are those magical immortality pears?

CHORUS. This is Death.

She hates those fucking pears.

DEATH. I do! I do hate those fucking pears. You know, you don't have to waste my time like this. He's not going to die and I'm a busy woman.

> (DEATH *exits in a huff, carrying the bell to her side.* AMELIA *looks confused. The* CHORUS *exhales sharply and snaps in unison.*)

CHORUS. Live again.

> (*Slowly,* JOSHUA *gets up profusely bleeding from his head. She laughs.*)

JOSHUA. Are you fucking kidding me, Amelia?! That hammer hurts so much!!

> (AMELIA *brings the hammer down with a scream, sending him crashing down behind the table. Breathing heavy, she waits again.*)

> (*The bell sound again and* DEATH *enters. When she sees* AMELIA *she stops. She looks behind the table again and makes a sour face.*)

DEATH. Again? Please stop doing that. You're really screwing with my schedule and this bell is heavy. Look, you're just making the mess worse. Like I said, he's not going to die. And I'm getting really annoyed. You got me?

> (*She exits again. The* CHORUS *exhales sharply and snaps in unison.*)

CHORUS. Live again

(Slowly **JOSHUA** *gets up from behind the table, now covered in blood. There's probably a pool of blood forming at the base of the table.)*

AMELIA. Okay. Okay, okay. Okay, maybe this relationship can work. I'll stay.

JOSHUA. And you're just gonna bludgeon me with a hammer any time you get frustrated with our relationship?

AMELIA. Don't be silly. It doesn't have to be a hammer.

(He drags himself into the chair and eats as she sits down, drops the bloody hammer on the table, picks up a pear, and also takes a bite.)

CHORUS. This is Joshua eating a pear
Happy with his delicious choice
Trust us; his head really hurts

JOSHUA. I love you.

AMELIA. I love you, too.

(They kiss. It's messy.)

End of Play

Mrs. Evelyn Foxy & Her Low Orbit Anxiety

MRS. EVELYN FOXY & HER LOW ORBIT ANXIETY was commissioned and produced by City Theatre in Miami, Florida as a part of *Summer Shorts 2015* (John Manzelli, Producing Artistic Director and Susan Westfall, Literary Director) and premiered at the Adrienne Arsht Center for the Performing Arts on June 6, 2015. The production was directed by Paul Tei. The cast was as follows:

EVELYN...Elizabeth Dimon
MIKE...Bechir Sylvain
BARBARA .... Chasity Hart
BILLY ....Michael Uribe

CHARACTERS

EVELYN – a woman, very polite, a wonderful hostess, housebound due to a crippling fear with a serious & ridiculous historical precedent

MIKE – a man, a volunteer signature collector, trying to be a polite and optimistic prisoner

BARBARA – a woman, Evelyn's daughter, reconciled with the past and very frustrated with her mom

BILLY – a young man, very physically fit and eager, he's into landscaping and the universe

AUTHOR'S NOTES

Keraunothnetophobia is the (largely irrational) fear of being struck by falling man-made satellites.

There are around 1,100 operating satellites in orbit above the Earth. There are also 2,600 satellites that are no longer active.

When the "debris" falls from space, it will ideally fall from as high as possible and crash loudly. Unexpected & terrifying.

This all moves quickly. It's not thoughtful.

(**EVELYN FOXY** *is sitting in her living room having a cup of tea. She's well put together in slacks and a sweater, very comfy. She keeps checking her watch. There is a tea set on the coffee table.* **MIKE** *is across from her. He's in jeans and button-up shirt with a blue clipboard full of signatures on his lap.*)

EVELYN. So you say these owls are nocturnal, isn't that intriguing? They must have much better night vision than I do. I mean to tell you I just trip all over the place trying to get a glass of water in the dark.

(*She laughs.* **MIKE** *glances at the door again.*)

Did you need some more tea?

MIKE. Um...no thank you?

(*Suddenly* **BARBARA** *enters through the front door. She's in a skirt and suit jacket. Carrying a coat and purse. She looks all business.*)

BARBARA. Mom! Oh, you're right here.

EVELYN. Good morning, honey. I didn't know you'd be stopping by today.

BARBARA. I had some errands over this way before work so I thought I'd drop in.

(*She sets down her coat and purse.* **MIKE** *turns to* **BARBARA** *and quietly, urgently whispers.*)

MIKE. Help me.

EVELYN. You might have called first? What if I was out and about?

BARBARA. You're never out and about, Mom. Who is this man?

EVELYN. Oh, this is Mike.

BARBARA. Why is he whispering?

EVELYN. Maybe he has a condition?

BARBARA. Why is he asking for help?

EVELYN. Don't be silly. Mike, do you need help?

MIKE. Maybe?

EVELYN. Listen, Barbara, it's nothing for you to get involved in. Mike here showed up at the door asking if I care about the environment and of course I do so I invited him in and then he asked me if I knew anything about spotted owls and of course I don't so I invited him to tell me all about them over tea and to hopefully keep talking until around 9:07am Eastern Standard Time. I don't see what the big deal is?

BARBARA. Uh huh. And what happens at 9:07am Eastern Standard Time?

EVELYN. He…he can go outside again. Did you know spotted owls eat mice?

BARBARA. Mom.

EVELYN. They grab them up in their, um…?

MIKE. Talons.

EVELYN. Talons! Yes. Just crush their little bones.

BARBARA. Mom.

EVELYN. I'm being polite.

MIKE. She won't let me leave.

BARBARA. Mom! You're holding him hostage!

EVELYN. Oh Jesus, Barbara, you're always so dramatic. Mike, are you a hostage?

MIKE. I don't know, not technically.

EVELYN. There. You see?

MIKE. But every time I try to go to the door, she [jumps up and…]

EVELYN. [You know how] important hospitality is to me, Barbara.

BARBARA. Mom, it is not okay to subject people to your irrational fears.

EVELYN. Irrational?!

BARBARA. Yes, irrational. Irrational! It is ridiculous to keep this probably mentally handicapped volunteer signature collector [trapped in…]

MIKE. [I'm not mentally] handicapped.

BARBARA. Whatever, it's not okay to keep people prisoner because you're afraid something is going to fall out of the sky and kill them.

EVELYN. It's a nightmare.

> *(There is a sudden sting of melodramatic music as* **EVELYN** *puts her hand over her heart and looks to the skies dramatically.)*

BARBARA. Good grief.

EVELYN. There is no reason to mock my enduring pain, Barbara. I raised you to be a nice person. Not a jerk.

BARBARA. You raised me to think the sky is falling and it took me a really long time to realize that's [totally insane.]

EVELYN. [Oh, well, I'm so] sorry. I thought a mother's job was to keep her daughter safe and prepared and aware of the cruel, fickle world.

BARBARA. I feel like you could have made a bunt cake instead.

EVELYN. I did both!

MIKE. Well it was lovely meeting you, Mrs. Foxy. But I really [should be…]

EVELYN. [Now Mike, I] know I told you to call me Evelyn.

MIKE. Yes, Evelyn, of course. I really should be going.

> *(***EVELYN*** *rushes to the door with urgency, pushing* **BARBARA** *out of the way and bracing against it.)*

BARBARA. Mom!

EVELYN. Barbara, hush.

BARBARA. Just let him leave.

EVELYN. He can leave. Of course. I just want to say something first. Okay? Mike, I don't think you understand how very much I want to save the, um, what

was it? The spotted owl! And that means people like you
have to continue doing your good work. But how, Mike,
how will you continue to do your good work on behalf
of those endangered spotted owls if you're crushed
to death by a falling piece of a telecommunications
satellite that happens to be roughly overhead for the
next few minutes? Have you thought about that, Mike?
That's a real question, please answer.

BARBARA. Mike, my mother suffers from a relatively
extreme case of keraunothnetophobia.

MIKE. Kerauno...?

BARBARA. Keraunothnetophobia. It's the fear of falling man
made satellites and it is ridiculous and embarrassing.

EVELYN. I'm standing right here, Barbara.

(She turns to her mother.)

BARBARA. It is ridiculous and embarrassing.

EVELYN. Keraunothnetophobia is nothing to scoff at, thank
you.

BARBARA. Keraunothnetophobia is a winning Scrabble
play, not something that should control your life. Or
my life. Or poor disabled Mike's life!

MIKE. I'm not disabled.

EVELYN. If only your father was here.

(There is a sudden sting of melodramatic music as
EVELYN *puts her hand over her heart and looks to*
the skies dramatically.)

BARBARA. Don't do it, Mom.

EVELYN. If only he and our prize-winning King Charles
Cavalier Spaniel Duchess hadn't been out walking that
crisp fall morning. If only he hadn't stopped to let
Duchess smell the freshly planted flowers. If only he
hadn't been unaware of the over 1500 active satellites
up there not to mention the 2600 dead satellites left as
floating junk in orbit just waiting for the right moment
to reenter the atmosphere careening back to earth with
deadly force. If only he hadn't been crushed, along

with Duchess, at the corner of Elm and 7th Street by super-heated, metallic space debris.

MIKE. Oh my God!

BARBARA. Oh please, don't encourage her.

MIKE. Your dad was crushed by falling space debris?

EVELYN. Our lovely, high-spirited King Charles Spaniel Duchess was crushed, too.

BARBARA. Kind of puts the whole spotted owl thing in perspective, huh?

MIKE. How can you be so callous?

BARBARA. Calm down, Mike, it didn't happen to you. I was just a little kid and she's only bringing it up right now to keep you inside until her illegal satellite-tracking app tells her the sky is clear. Where's the iPad, Mom.

EVELYN. I deleted that app.

BARBARA. I don't believe you.

EVELYN. The iPad is in the kitchen, check for yourself.

(**BARBARA** *begins to walk towards the kitchen.*)

Fine! Fine. I didn't delete it. And thank goodness I didn't because if I wasn't keeping an eye out then poor, simple Mike might have been killed.

MIKE. This is really making me think about my own mortality.

BARBARA. Shut-up, Mike. Mom, seriously, can we please just let him leave and have a nice visit?

EVELYN. You know, now might be a good time to mention that I don't like how you just drop in unannounced, Barbara. It's quite rude.

BARBARA. I thought it would be nice to see you before work. You know I worry.

EVELYN. Well, maybe I had other things to do.

BARBARA. Okay. You don't want me to visit?

EVELYN. Oh, I don't know, Barbara. Sometimes I just hate your face.

BARBARA. Wait, excuse me?

EVELYN. That sour, pinched face. Always so sure you know what's best for everyone else. Always so quick to jump into other people's business. You're my daughter and I love you but it just exhausts me. I'm just living my life and it somehow constantly offends you. Maybe if you had some things going on in your own life, you wouldn't be so concerned about me.

BARBARA. Mom!

EVELYN. Well, I don't know. It's just a theory.

> *(There's a knock at the door.* EVELYN *opens it to reveal* BILLY, *the good natured young man who cuts all the lawns in the neighborhood as a way of avoiding community college, sweaty in nothing but running shorts and sneakers. She grabs him by the arm and pulls him inside.)*

BILLY. Hey, Evelyn! Whoa. Must be dangerous out there today, huh?

BARBARA. You can't just keep dragging people into the house!

BILLY. Oh, wow! Barbara? It's been, like, forever. It's me, Billy. Come on, you fully used to babysit when I was little. And you would watch my parents' Cinemax when you thought I was in bed.

BARBARA. Oh, I don't [think that...]

BILLY. [It's cool, I never] told on you. Anyway, now I do yard work for all the neighbors so my folks will stay off my back about college. But I dig it.

EVELYN. Billy, this is Mike. He wants to save the owls.

BILLY. Cool. Hey.
So Evelyn, are we not, like, having our session this morning or...?

BARBARA. What session?

EVELYN. None of your business.

BARBARA. Ugh. Fine. Billy, what session?

BILLY. Oh, so like every Tuesday morning after my run, I come over here and your Mom and I use her iPad to track satellites up in the space. We're, like, really into the universe.

EVELYN. Because Billy understands me.

> *(The sting of melodramatic music.* EVELYN *puts her hand over her heart and looks to the skies.* BILLY *puts his hand to his heart and his free arm around* EVELYN. *He looks up to the exact same place.)*

BARBARA. Oh my God.

BILLY. And then I use the shower and we talk about how ephemeral and fleeting life can be during like usually two or three hours of amazing tantric sex.

BARBARA. What?!

MIKE. Wow.

BARBARA. Shut the fuck up, Mike!

BILLY. It's like so connected and focused and just hot. But like really hot. Most times I end up totally dehydrated.

BARBARA. Please stop.

EVELYN. Knowing that you could die at any moment by being crushed by something rocketing down from the heavens really invigorates every little choice, Barbara. Every little moment. And the big moments, too.

> *(*EVELYN *winks at* BILLY. *He laughs, embarrassed.)*

BARBARA. I thought you were a terrified shut in?

EVELYN. Oh, Honey, that's only because I don't share things with you because you're judgmental and my life is none of your business. I'm your mom but I have my own life and you don't suddenly know what's best for me just because you think you're an adult. I've been an adult a lot longer than you and I've seen things. A lot of things. So many things.

BARBARA. This is insane. I'm going. I have to go.

> *(*BARBARA *grabs her purse and her coat and heads for the door.)*

EVELYN. Oh no! Please don't go out there yet, Barbara. For once in your life listen to me and wait a few more minutes. Just to be safe. What can it hurt?

> (**BARBARA** *throws open the door.* **MIKE** *stands up like he might bolt.*)

BARBARA. Look out there, Mom! It's fine. It's safe. Nothing is going to happen. You may have constructed a little world in here for yourself complete with tea parties, bootleg NORAD tracking systems, and barely legal boys, sorry Billy, but I will not enable this fear. I will not be a part of making this situation okay. I will not. I won't! So good luck to you, Mike. Good luck to you, Billy. And Mom, you won't have to worry about me just dropping by anymore because it seems very clear that –

> (*A piece of space debris [think toaster or some other appliance-sized piece of metal] falls from high up onto the stage outside the front door with a crash, cutting* **BARBARA** *off and terrifying everyone. Everything is still. Heavy breathing.* **MIKE** *slowly sits back down.*)

EVELYN. Billy, let's have a cup of tea before we kick everyone out. Barbara, would you care to join us for some tea or are you still storming out in a huff?

> (**BARBARA**, *shell-shocked, drops her purse and her coat, leaves the door open, walks back over, and sits down.* **EVELYN** *pours tea.*)

Now see? A little healthy fear and everyone's just fine. Like I always say, you just never know. Barbara, drink your tea before it gets cold.

End of Play

Niagara Falls
a play in two parts

NIAGARA FALLS was commissioned by Melissa Y. Smith for the American Conservatory Theatre Graduate Acting Company. A workshop production opened on December 13, 2012 in the Hastings Studio Theater in San Francisco, California. The production was directed by Melissa Y. Smith. Sarah Pykett was the Production Designer. The Production Stage Manager was Shannon Reilly. The cast was as follows:

AVERY	Josie Alvarez
JACK	Elvin McRae
LINDA	Dominique Salerno
BEN	Jarrod Smith
MAY	Kemiyondo Coutinho
TOBY	Ryan Williams French
BALE	Ben Quinn
MAX	Rafael Jordan
ESSA	Stefanée Martin
CLIFF	Glenn Stott
JANE	Danielle Frimer
DAN	Joel Bernard

NIAGARA FALLS premiered at Theatre of NOTE in Los Angeles, California on February 22, 2015. It was produced by John Colella and Reamy Hall. The production was directed by Ryan Bergmann with sets by Tristan Jeffers, costumes by Sarah Figoten Wilson, lights by Matthew Brian Denman, sound by Rebecca Kessen, and properties by Michael O'Hara. The Production Stage Manager was Kelly Egan. The cast was as follows:

AVERY	Alina Phelan
JACK	John Colella
LINDA	Kathey Deitch
BEN	Trevor H Olsen
MAY	Debbie Jaffe
TOBY	Alexis DeLaRosa
BALE	Garett Maggart
MAX	Travis York
ESSA	Jenny Soo
CLIFF	Travis Moscinski
JANE	Reamy Hall
DAN	Brad C Light

CHARACTERS

PART ONE

"LONELY HONEYMOON"

AVERY – a new wife, upbeat, but unsure she's made the right decision & a anxious about what's been left behind; she looks a lot like Jane

JACK – a new husband, cocky, fun, impetuous, not very serious, and definitely the captain of his own ship

BEN – a man, faithful and romantic, fighting both a losing battle to save his marriage and a looming loneliness

MAY – a woman, Ben's wife, a bit ferocious, completely done with the past and ready for something new

TOBY – a man, May's new fling, takes things as they come and has a no nonsense, no regrets approach to love

LINDA – a woman, a crack concierge, goes above and beyond, she always brings the champagne

PART TWO

"FORTUNETELLERS & DAREDEVILS"

BALE – a man, nomadic, a "carnie," but the fun kind of carnie, a touch of mystical wisdom; he's not creepy

MAX – a man, a pretty down to earth guy just trying to get over his failures. By burning everything down.

CLIFF – a man, not easily taken in by con artists, not really looking for answers - but they're looking for him

ESSA – a woman, a fortuneteller, well... the niece of a fortuneteller who may or may not be for real

DAN – a man, a guy's guy, a real daredevil; that's his profession, he performs daredevil stunts for a living

JANE – a woman, an amnesiac, Jane Doe, starting fresh with wide eyes, she might have survived the unthinkable; she looks a lot like Avery

AUTHOR'S NOTES

[ ] indicate overlapping dialogue

The **Foley Ensemble** in Act One (comprised of the Act Two company) remains seated on stage for the entire act, off to one side. They provide all **sound effects** and **music cues** live during performance. No instruments; all vocals and percussion. Maybe an ocarina of some sort if really needed for flavor somewhere. There should be no pre-recorded sound/music in the act.

Ideally this ensemble will wear ponchos or slickers reminiscent of the iconic Niagara Falls "Maid of the Mists" boat rides.

During the **INTERVAL** between acts, the group dance begins set against live music provided by the Foley Ensemble. As more actors join the dance and it grows, there is a transition to pre-recorded music. By the end of the interval, all of the actors are dancing, including the Foley Ensemble (having put their chairs away) and a transition is made from live sound to recorded sound. All sound moving forward in Act Two will be comprised of recorded cues.

TECH: During the quick blackout near the end of Part 2, the water in Linda's buckets should be poured onto Avery and Dan. Quickly drenching them without leaving the stage.

The setting should all be very simple, very representative. Nothing too fully realized is necessary. Key pieces.

Part One is set in the living area of a Honeymoon suite in a Niagara Falls hotel; a mid-level affair. The "stain" in the carpet should be indicated by something resembling the chalk outline of a body. Probably white tape, but whatever is easiest. But at the very least it should be vaguely body-shaped, enough to recognize.

Part Two is set in three different areas of in a carnival along the Niagara Falls boardwalk. The only element necessary on stage is a single white canvas, nothing too large, where simple shadow images are specified to project location. And some strand lights.

The play should ideally be relatively fleet and, including the interval, flow through as a seamless evening. **No intermission.**

PART ONE

Lonely Honeymoon

(The lounge area of a classy honeymoon suite in a still middle-of-the-road hotel overlooking Niagara Falls. **AVERY** *looks out the window, dressed and ready to tackle the day. She takes in the view.)*

(She slides the balcony door open a bit. **The sounds of raging, churning water** *rush in. She closes the door with a smile, sealing the sounds outside.)*

(She slides the balcony door again, only more. **The sounds of raging, churning water** *rush in. She lets the cold and noise hug her before closing the door again.)*

*(***JACK*** enters in pajama pants, no shirt, probably still bed head. He has a mug of coffee.)*

JACK. Hello there, Mrs. Perch.

(They kiss.)

AVERY. That still sounds funny. "Mrs. Perch." "Mrs. [Perch.]"

JACK. [You'll get] used to it.

AVERY. "Mrs. Perch." I don't know, I suppose. Maybe it's not that it sounds funny, maybe it just sounds weird. It doesn't matter, who's ever going to call me that anyway?

JACK. Lots of people. Mrs. Avery Perch. Wife of Jack Perch. Happy couple.

AVERY. Ah. Well…it's really an amazing view, isn't it?

JACK. That's kind of the point I think.

AVERY. You haven't even looked.

JACK. It's not going anywhere.

AVERY. And it's so loud.

> (*She slides the balcony door open.* **The sounds of raging, churning water** *rush in. They have to speak over them.* **JACK** *immediately recoils a bit from the chill.*)

If you open the balcony door, it's loud.

JACK. Then let's keep it closed, it's chilly out there anyway.

AVERY. We came here for the wonder of the natural beauty, right?

> (*She closes the balcony door.*)

You're such a spoilsport, wait, why aren't you ready?

JACK. What's the rush?

AVERY. We have a lot planned today, Mr. Perch.

JACK. I still need to get cleaned up.

AVERY. Go.

JACK. Is this how it's gonna be for our entire marriage? You trying to plan every little thing?

AVERY. Go.

JACK. I will, Avery, just… I want your opinion on something.

AVERY. I need us to go get coffee before you ask my opinion on anything.

JACK. I already have coffee. So there's this…look at me.

> (*She does.*)

It's gonna sound odd.

AVERY. Great.

JACK. I moved that cushy chair in the little sitting area. The one [with the…]

AVERY. [Jesus, Jack,] why are you moving the hotel furniture?

JACK. I was going to surprise you by positioning it in the middle of the room so I could do this whole "naked king" routine.

AVERY. Huh. I'm sorry that didn't work out.

JACK. Me too. But that's not, wait, you would've liked that?

AVERY. Maybe.

JACK. Good to know. But I didn't get that far because there was something under the chair. This kind of shadow thing on the carpet.

AVERY. A kind of shadow thing?

JACK. A stain.

AVERY. If you mean "stain" just say, "stain." It really drives me crazy the way you overcomplicate things sometimes. "Stain." They probably put the chair there to cover it up.

JACK. Obviously.

AVERY. So then put the chair back, you can do the king thing later. I'll still like it and act scandalized or whatever turns you on.

JACK. Don't think I won't, but again that's not the point. It's a big stain. And we're paying a lot of money for this room.

AVERY. My parents are paying a lot of money for this room.

JACK. Oh. That's what we're doing?

AVERY. I'm not doing anything.

JACK. They insisted on paying for it.

AVERY. They were in shock and didn't have time to buy a present.

JACK. I can afford to give us a honeymoon.

AVERY. I know. I love you. I haven't had coffee yet.

JACK. I love you, too. Do you want some of my coffee?

AVERY. Thank you.

JACK. It has Bailey's in it.

AVERY. Then no. Good grief.

JACK. Well, I'm anxious, okay? A little. I'm not afraid to say I'm anxious. It's our honeymoon and I feel like it should have a certain vibe and I don't want to be tense. And we did kind of rush into all of this, so there's bound to be more "getting to know you" and I don't want [that to...]

AVERY. [Wait, you] don't think we made a mistake, [do you?]

JACK. [Whoa, whoa,] whoa, no I do not. No one said anything about a mistake. Fast is not a mistake. Fast just means more to discover.

AVERY. But you said "anxious."

JACK. I said "a little." That's so completely normal.

AVERY. Okay, right. Yes. Come on, who cares about a silly stain on the carpet? Just cover it up and it'll be like it's not there. We have an entire itinerary to get through today and we've already probably missed the continental breakfast because you slept so late.

JACK. We slept late. Together. We both did that.

AVERY. Mm hm. And then we woke up and I got ready and then took some time to enjoy this stunning view of the falls while you played with furniture. Now chop chop, things to do.

JACK. So we should both go ahead and acknowledge that it was unrealistic to think the morning after our wedding [that we'd...]

AVERY. [For the] record, you said you didn't want to waste a minute of this honeymoon.

JACK. I meant I wanted to have a lot of sex.

AVERY. And we did. And we will some more. And this part in between, I want to walk around and have amazing food and ride on the overlook boat thing in raincoats and walk by the falls.

JACK. The thing about the stain in the carpet [though is...]

AVERY. [Oh my] God, I will drown you in that garden tub, so help me.

JACK. The thing about the stain is that it's "person shaped."

        (*Pause.*)

AVERY. What does that mean?

JACK. It means it's, how is that unclear? The stain is shaped like a person. Kind of like a person.

AVERY. Oh no, I can't believe I married you. I actually just felt this ring get tighter [on my finger.]

JACK. [Like someone] decided to lie down on the floor and then never got up. Just faded away leaving a stain. Or melted. No, that's weird, let's go with faded away. And then the hotel staff put a chair on it.

(He waits for reaction...)

And I want you to look at it.

AVERY. Why?

JACK. Maybe I'm wrong.

AVERY. Wrong?

JACK. Maybe it's like a cloud and it looks different to everyone who sees it. Maybe you'll see a train or a tiny horse or something?

AVERY. Instead of a person.

JACK. Or a bicycle.

AVERY. Instead of a dead person.

JACK. I didn't say a dead person; I said a body.

AVERY. Presumably belonging to a person.

JACK. Who isn't necessarily dead; just look at it.

AVERY. Jack. I'm standing here in the presence of the most beautiful natural wonder in the world and you want me to look at a...

(He waits expectantly.)

Fine. But I swear to you that if I find out my mother was right and you're a complete imbecile then I am going to be so mad.

JACK. Your mother loves me.

AVERY. Oh God, really?

JACK. Doesn't she?

AVERY. No.

*(He moves a comfy-looking chair, he points to the outline in tape of a body shape on the floor. As the stain is revealed, **a quiet hissing or humming sneaks** into the room. It's almost like a bottle or soda being opened and then it slowly fades away.)*

JACK. You see it?

(She stares.)

Do you see it?

AVERY. Of course I see it.

JACK. And...?

AVERY. And what? And put the chair back.

JACK. Avery.

AVERY. Put the chair back. We'll go get breakfast.

(She crosses back to the windows.)

JACK. What could leave a stain like that?

AVERY. Jack. A person. A dead person, are you happy? It really clearly looks like there was a body here and it started to decompose and the hotel people found it and took it away and tried to clean up the mess but couldn't get the stain out and now it looks like this. So they put a chair on it, sprayed some air freshener, and crossed their fingers.

JACK. Whoa.

AVERY. Why is this my honeymoon? Let's ask the front desk to switch rooms.

JACK. This is the honeymoon suite.

AVERY. This is a honeymoon suite, not the only honeymoon suite.

JACK. But you love the view.

AVERY. The entire hotel faces this direction.

JACK. It's such a hassle to move everything.

AVERY. It's two suitcases.

JACK. This is my fault. You're blowing this stain out of proportion, but it's my fault. I'm sorry I brought it up. This is like when I told you I've been married before.

AVERY. You told me that last night.

JACK. Let's not backtrack. I know, pretend I never noticed the stain and just start this morning over. "Good, morning, Avery. You look beautiful and I can't believe I was lucky enough to marry you."

AVERY. In the interest of that "getting to know you" stuff, why exactly was it so important to show me this?

JACK. We're supposed to share everything. It was curious to me.

AVERY. "Dear Mom, it turns out you were right about Jack."

JACK. Look, I'm putting the chair back, okay? There. It's all covered up.

(He puts the chair back.)

AVERY. It's kind of covered up.

JACK. It's as covered up as it's going to get.

AVERY. I hate it.

JACK. Fine, we can try to switch rooms. I'll ask.

AVERY. Thank you.

JACK. I'm sorry I made you look at it.

AVERY. Ugh, it's… I'm just being stupid about it. I overreact sometimes. You know that. Well, you should know that, I suppose. Also, I just really don't like dead things. At all. You should know that too. Or wet plaster. Or drug addicts.

JACK. Drug addicts? You mean like serious drug addicts.

AVERY. I mean drug addiction generally; it scares me.

JACK. But you mean like heroin, right? Or meth? Heavy stuff. Not Aderal or Xanax or that kind of low-key, everyday [kind of…]

AVERY. [Why? Is there] something I should know?

JACK. No. What? I mean, it's not like I, no, I won't casually use any of those on the weekends sometimes when we go out, so it's not a problem.

AVERY. Oh God.

JACK. And what's wrong with wet plaster?

AVERY. It sounds squishy. Look, just go get cleaned up and by the time we have some food I won't care about the stain anymore. Probably.

JACK. You're very sexy, Mrs. Perch.

AVERY. Right now I'm more disturbed than anything.

JACK. When I tell you that you're sexy, you're going to need to believe it. That's something you should know about me. I'm not gonna lie to you, not about that. Not about anything, but definitely not about that. Because you are always sexy. Oh, and I don't like sushi or dancing.

AVERY. Oh no, but I love to dance.

JACK. We'll figure it out.

> *(He kisses her. There is a knock and* **LINDA** *enters without waiting and talks without really listening. She is in a skirt, a sharp jacket and she carries a champagne bottle. She might actually be nice, but it's hard to tell through all of the "acting nice.")*

LINDA. Knock, knock, good morning!

JACK. Uh…good morning?

LINDA. Linda. Linda Imelda. I work in guest services and I wanted to stop by and drop off this champagne. Congratulations. On the wedding. On being married. I hope I didn't wake you. Nope, just look at you all ready to tackle the day. Well mostly ready, she might be a little more ready than you. Oh, I know it's early, but I hate when they don't prepare the honeymoon suites in advance. Feels a bit like I have to do just about everything sometimes.

AVERY. That's so thoughtful, thank you.

JACK. Sure, [thanks.]

LINDA. [And you] must be Mr. and Mrs. Perch.

AVERY. It just sounds weird, doesn't it?

JACK. No.

LINDA. Oh, look, you have an amazing view from this room, don't you? Breathtaking. Between us, it's the best view in the place. It's almost hypnotic, with the sound and

the rushing water. Oh, but don't stare too long. That's
my honeymoon advice. Well, keep a few secrets from
each other so the mystery is still alive. That's my actual
honeymoon advice. But also, don't stare too long at the
falls. You'll start to see things; that's what I hear anyway.
People see strange things when they look for too long.

AVERY. What kind of things?

LINDA. Ha! Better to get out there and walk around anyway,
right? Who wants to be cooped up inside?

JACK. I should get dressed. Thanks for the champagne.

> (*He kisses* AVERY's *cheek and disappears from the
> room.*)

LINDA. Aw, I love when we have newlyweds. It's so cute and
inspiring. I was a newlywed once. Not so long ago. No,
really, just a few years.

AVERY. Oh, that's wonderful.

LINDA. It's amazing how much can change in such a short
period of time.

AVERY. Oh. Are you still married?

LINDA. Let's not talk about me, all of my silliness.

AVERY. Is that a "no?"

LINDA. Let's not talk about me and unhappy, awful things
or lost dreams. All the things I could have been if not
for the heart's folly.

AVERY. Wow.

LINDA. Yes. So how are you enjoying the room?

AVERY. Actually, we were going to ask about…no, it's all
fine.

LINDA. Fine?

AVERY. Better than fine. Wonderful.

LINDA. You were going to say something else.

AVERY. It's really not important.

LINDA. Please, tell me. It's my job to make this experience
unforgettable for you both, to start your life off
together with panache. And perhaps somehow

vicariously experience the joy I should have had as a married woman before everything went sour so quickly. I take it all very seriously. I even brought champagne.

AVERY. I thought the champagne was from the hotel?

LINDA. It's from both of us.

AVERY. Okay. Well, it's really not a problem, but there's a stain of some kind on the carpet and it's a bit disconcerting.

LINDA. Oh no, that's inexcusable, and on your honeymoon. Where is it?

AVERY. Just over here. Underneath this chair. It's not hurting anything, but now that we know it's here, it's kind of difficult to ignore.

> (**AVERY** *pulls the chair out of the way revealing the outline. As the stain is revealed,* **a quiet hissing or humming sneaks** *into the room. Again, it's almost like a bottle or soda being opened and slowly fades away.* **LINDA** *looks at it in disbelief. Then that turns into frustrated anger.)*

LINDA. You know, it's beyond me. Really. I scrubbed this stain myself until it was completely gone.

AVERY. Did you?

LINDA. So frustrating. I'll be back with some soapy water and an industrial strength cleaner or two to take care of it once and for all.

AVERY. Oh, no, you really don't have to [do that.]

LINDA. [Oh, no, I] absolutely do. In the meantime, I'd advise you not to touch.

AVERY. Why shouldn't I touch it?

LINDA. Clearly that's some stubborn grime. Enjoy the champagne.

> (**LINDA** *exits with purpose.* **AVERY** *examines the stain. She bends over and touches it. The moment her fingers make contact, the lights shift and* **a chorus of mixed, overlapping, and hushed conversations fills the room.** *She pulls her hand away and it all stops immediately.)*

(She looks around. She gingerly reaches out and tries again. The light shift. **The chorus returns, as if someone just cracked the door to a secret party and the sound is escaping.** *She pulls her hand away and places it over her heart.* **For a moment, while her hand is there, we can hear her heart beating hard, excited in the silence.** *There's something to this. She lies down next to the stain on her side and places her hand on the area where the "hand" of the stain might be and closes her eyes.)*

(The lights shift. **The sound begins, hushed, but rises quickly to full volume and then even louder and then, just as quickly vanishes with an intense exhale as...)**

*(***LINDA** *leads* **BEN** *into the room. He has an overnight bag. She is already talking, as if the pair had materialized from the overlapping sounds.)*

I have to say, in all the years I've worked here, this is one of the loveliest surprises.

BEN. I really appreciate it.

LINDA. No, no, I'm so glad I could be a part of it.

BEN. That's nice.

LINDA. And what anniversary is this?

BEN. It's our tenth. We planned this whole trip, but I had to work at the last minute. I've been so busy lately, not even busy, just consumed by other things.

LINDA. Consumed. What an evocative word.

BEN. I suppose it is. Anyway, she has no idea I made the time to actually show up here.

LINDA. She's going to be so surprised!

BEN. That's right.

LINDA. I love it. And thank goodness, because this is our honeymoon suite and it would be such a shame to stay in it alone, wouldn't it?

BEN. Such a shame. I'll tell you, when she said she was still coming on her own, I half didn't believe her.

LINDA. She sounds like a real pistol. Oh, did you see the view?

(BEN *and* LINDA *move to the windows.*)

BEN. It's breathtaking.

LINDA. That's just how I describe it. So grand. It can actually start to make a person feel small, not in a bad way you understand, but small in the face of larger things.

BEN. No, I understand what you mean.

LINDA. Ah, don't stare at it too long though. It'll make you start to see things.

BEN. Like what?

LINDA. Oh, when will she be back? Your wife?

BEN. No idea. I assumed she'd be here curled up with a book. She does that. She's a voracious reader. Oh, and she also carves little figurines out of soap.

LINDA. Oh, isn't that…delightful.

BEN. Little lambs and kittens. It's just that she'll probably clean out all of your little complimentary soaps.

LINDA. Well, they are complimentary.

BEN. She might be at dinner. I suppose it's that time, [isn't it?]

LINDA. [Oh! I bet I] have time to grab some champagne for you. Would that be good? That would be good, wouldn't it?

BEN. That would be perfect.

LINDA. Oh, I love romance. I sacrificed so much in life for romance only to have it callously abandon my heart on a small raft buffeted by the unforgiving sea. But who has time for reverie and horrific sadness? I need to get you that champagne. I'll be back soon.

(LINDA *exits with purpose.* BEN *takes a small stuffed bear with a red ribbon around its neck out of his travel bag and positions it on the chair.*

*He looks out the windows at the view. Something
catches his attention. He leans in and tries to
see more as **a harmonious tone fills the space. It
begins to bend pitch into a discordant noise** as
BEN steps away from the window. **At its peak, the
sound abruptly stops with a jolt or a pop.**)*

BEN. What in the hell…?

(**LINDA** *returns, out of breath and carrying
champagne.*)

LINDA. Is it too late? Should I yell surprise?

BEN. No, no, you're fine. I just…

LINDA. Oh no. I know that look, that dazed look. You were
staring out the window weren't you?

BEN. Only for a minute. And it does make you see things.

LINDA. That was quick. Are you particularly susceptible to
suggestion? It doesn't matter; forget about whatever
you saw. It's all just a trick of the light.

BEN. I thought I saw someone go over the falls?

LINDA. Mm hm. Sometimes daredevils go over in barrels.
One jumped off the bridge. It's all perfectly safe, well
not perfectly. Oh, I should have brought nice glasses.

BEN. I know this sounds insane, but I could've sworn it
was me. I saw myself in the water, washed over the falls.
How do you like that?

LINDA. I really cannot stress to you enough all the ways
that you should not give whatever you just saw another
thought.

BEN. I feel a little queasy.

LINDA. It'll pass.

BEN. You don't think that sounds crazy?

LINDA. Who can say? I gave up my dream of singing opera
professionally for a woman who abandoned me here to
follow her own dream of swimming the North Atlantic.

BEN. Oh my God.

LINDA. She vanished in the freezing waves.

BEN. Oh my God.

LINDA. It sounds awful, doesn't it? That's only because it is.

BEN. Okay, that is terribly unfortunate. And sad. And...it's also a lot to share with a stranger.

LINDA. Oh, I'm sorry. I'm bad with boundaries. Now, when you saw yourself go over the falls, were you in a barrel?

BEN. No.

LINDA. Well, that does sound crazy, but purely from a safety standpoint. They say the barrels take the sting out of the landing. Who knows? I'll go get some glasses.

> *(Suddenly* MAY *crashes through the door.* BEN *starts to say something but stops because* MAY *is in a passionate frenzy with* TOBY, *hands and mouths everywhere. She doesn't look like a woman who carves little figurines out of soap.* LINDA *freezes awkwardly.)*

MAY. Oh my God, [yes.]

TOBY. [Who takes] care of you better than me?

MAY. No one, Toby. [No one.]

TOBY. [That's right,] baby.

MAY. You are the best part of my vacation.

TOBY. Oh, I know that's right.

> *(This goes on for longer than it should until...)*

BEN. May.

> *(*MAY *and* TOBY *suddenly break apart, startled.)*

MAY. Ben! What are...what are you doing here?!

BEN. I came to surprise you.

LINDA. With champagne.

BEN. What the hell [is this?]

TOBY. [Oh, this is] the husband.

BEN. Yes, I am the God damn husband, who [are you?]

MAY. [Just give me] a minute, Toby.

> *(She pushes* BEN *back towards the windows in some kind of attempt to separate the men.)*

LINDA. I'll get those glasses.

> (**LINDA** *exits quickly.*)

MAY. What glasses? Who was that?

BEN. Tell me why I shouldn't take this guy apart, May?

TOBY. You're welcome to try, my friend.

BEN. I'm not your friend.

> (*He tries to make a move for* **TOBY**, *but* **MAY** *pushes him back. Hard.*)

MAY. No. No! And Toby, I asked for a minute.

> (**TOBY** *shrugs, casually takes a blow pop out of this pocket, unwraps it and pops it into his mouth.*)

Ben, you can't take him apart because he would really hurt you and, more importantly, this isn't his fault.

BEN. He better wipe that smug smile off his face before I do.

TOBY. The smile is not for you, my friend. I just like the taste of something sweet on the tongue.

> (**BEN** *pushes past* **MAY** *and grapples* **TOBY** *to the floor.* **Percussive sounds punctuate the action** *as the men wrestle around.* **BEN** *tries to throw punches and really attack* **TOBY**, *but* **TOBY** *works to restrain him. It's not aggressive; it's very matter of fact. Meanwhile…*)

MAY. Ben, get off of him before you hurt yourself! You're not listening to me, this is my fault, I brought him here! I brought him because I wanted to come here with him. Not you. Not you!

> (**TOBY** *rolls an exhausted* **BEN** *away onto the floor.*)

Ben, will you please stop so we can have a conversation like thinking adults? Just sit there. Oh, your lip is going to swell. I'll get some ice.

> (*She goes to the ice bucket. Empty. She sighs in frustration.*)

Ugh. Toby, have we even seen an ice machine? Never mind, I'll be right back. Stay away from each other.

> (**TOBY** *holds up his hands in compliance. She exits.*)

TOBY. You are strong, my friend.

BEN. I'm not your fucking friend.

TOBY. Ah, okay. But may I say, I think that you grow tired so quickly because you're fighting for a hopeless cause.

BEN. You're talking about my marriage, you asshole.

TOBY. Your marriage, yes, yes, and do you love May?

BEN. Yes.

TOBY. Ah, you don't think about your answer before you say it, so it's just, what? Some kind of habit, something you've told yourself. That's not love. Love is thoughtful and makes you feel like a giant. Love finds you [no matter…]

BEN. [Don't think I] won't try to hit you again.

> (**TOBY** *chuckles.*)

TOBY. In my humble opinion, you may regret that, my friend.

BEN. What the fuck do you know about regret?

TOBY. More then you may think. Everyone carries regret. In fact, May has told me that you are full of it. This must weigh you down, slow you down, as regret is so heavy. In my opinion, it is the only thing to fear.

BEN. That's incredibly fucking naïve.

TOBY. Ah, but that does not mean I'm wrong.

BEN. Foreclosure, taxes, hypertension, hit and run accidents, terrorist attacks, deranged drug addicts, cutting your thumb off with a steak knife, strange vaguely foreign lotharios seducing your wife, there are all kinds of things to be afraid of in this world besides regret.

TOBY. Mmhm. And how does it feel to fear all of these things?

BEN. You sound like a fucking therapist.

TOBY. So you find me insightful? Thank you for that.

BEN. Jesus, that's not what I said. Can you just, just shut your mouth?

TOBY. I know it does not feel good. I know as sure as I'm sitting here, as sure as this candy tastes sweet, that all of those fears feel like a rope around your neck.

(The lights shift, soften, and perhaps a bit of color seeps in **as music reminiscent of a carnival or fair comes from somewhere far away.***)*

And you drag them. You drag them with you. So heavy that they begin to make you make decisions about your life, about your wife, about anything, that you do not wish to make. I may be the last man you want to hear this from, and I understand, but you should listen. Imagine a man, much like myself, riding on a carnival ride, some simple thing, but high in the air. A Ferris wheel, I think is what you'd call it. Imagine riding it with the woman you love as she tells you she does not feel special anymore, she does not love you anymore. You were not ready to hear it, you did not expect it, you were busy thinking of other things. You did not see her. And imagine that just as the words leave her lips, the ride stops and you a left there, hanging with her in this tiny car, waiting in space for the ride to begin again, quiet, broken, without language, sitting so close to her that you can not help but touch even though she has never been further away. And she will not look at you. And you cannot look at her. Imagine that is your goodbye. And it lasts and lasts because the ride is broken and for hours you say nothing. And then, as the ride begins again and your car moves towards the ground, just as you're almost back on your feet, she finally looks at you and says, "I wish you had said something to make me change my mind." And suddenly there is nothing but regret, nothing but regret and her face and carnival music that does not fit. So you see, my friend, you are not the first man who has suddenly found himself alone because mundane things have pulled his attention away.

> *(It's not a place he wants to remember or revisit and so he runs back quickly to now. The **music stops abruptly** as he shakes it off.)*

But I will not burden you with this story. That man learned to appreciate the here and now and you should do the same.

BEN. I'm nothing like the guy in your story, I came here to be with May. I came here to do the things that guy didn't.

TOBY. You are funny, my friend.

BEN. Fuck you.

TOBY. Ah, I see.

BEN. Listen, if I need a life lesson from someone, I can guarantee it's not you. It's definitely not you.

TOBY. Because I seduced your wife.

BEN. Yes.

TOBY. But you see, it did not happen as you imagine. She seduced me. And she did it well. With her laugh, with her smile, with the way she looks right into my eyes and asks for what she wants.

> *(The **percussive sounds** return as **BEN** grapples at **TOBY** again and again **TOBY** subdues him, this time holding him down.)*

I don't expect you to listen to me. Especially in this moment. But if you truly love May and she does not love you back, then why chase her? You will only grow to regret that choice. Instead, find another who will love you back and hold that woman close.

BEN. Can you please just shut your mouth?

TOBY. As you wish my friend. But you must take this opportunity to really see her. That is all.

> *(He rolls off of **BEN**, opens another blow pop, and puts it in his mouth. **MAY** returns with ice in a hand towel. She puts it on **BEN**'s lip. He flinches.)*

MAY. Toby, go do something somewhere else, please.

TOBY. He is a very stubborn man, May. And he thinks he loves you very much.

BEN. I do love her.

MAY. Toby, go.

TOBY. I know! I will get us all some flavored coffees. And I will make the flavor a surprise.

(*He exits.*)

MAY. I'm sorry.

BEN. That's the guy you're leaving me for?

MAY. No. Do you want some whiskey?

BEN. I can't believe you'd, ugh, "flavored coffee." You're leaving me for flavored coffee?

MAY. Don't be silly; I'm not leaving you for flavored coffee. I'll get some whiskey.

BEN. So you're not leaving me for him?

MAY. Is that all you can think about now?

BEN. I take time off from the office and show up here to surprise you because you seemed genuinely disappointed to come by yourself and because I love you and you're here with another guy, yes that's all I can think about.

MAY. I don't want to be cruel, but that one-track mind might be one of the biggest reasons I am, in fact, leaving you.

BEN. You just said [that you're...]

MAY. [I'm not] leaving you for Toby. Toby is fun and sexy and sees the world in a very unusual way. And that's good for me right now. But I'm leaving you for me, Ben. And it's not your fault. Exactly. We didn't really know each other when we got married and now you've changed, and me too. That's a thing that happened. We both changed into people that don't fit anymore.

BEN. I haven't changed.

(**MAY** *laughs.*)

I have not changed.

MAY. Ben.

BEN. May.

MAY. Ben.

BEN. May.

MAY. Ben, stop that. You've stopped being adventurous, okay? We were only together because of being adventurous.

BEN. Adventurous.

MAY. And not in a teenage girl, "I need danger" way. But we're just so predictable now.

BEN. I'm not fucking predictable.

MAY. I knew you would say that, so I beg to differ. You go to work, you come home, and that's all. You allow yourself to be completely overtaken by the smallest distractions, you bury yourself in work so you don't have to come home, and I know you don't do it on purpose, but I do know why you do it even if you don't. It's because you're bored and you don't know how to just be with me anymore. And I'm no better. I wander around our house all day doing God knows what, doing nothing, but... definitely not thinking of you.

BEN. Fantastic. How am I supposed to know you're unhappy? No seriously, don't scoff at that, how am I supposed to know?

MAY. Ben, I carve little figurines out of soap. That's not a normal hobby, that's how anxious people in prison whittle away their time.

BEN. I thought it made you happy.

MAY. Believe me, I know you thought that.

    (Pause.)

BEN. Happy anniversary.

MAY. Happy anniversary.

BEN. I shouldn't have come here.

MAY. Why? So you wouldn't have known? That might have been easier for now, but then I don't know how long it would've taken me to get up the courage to tell you.

BEN. You can tell me anything.

MAY. To get up the courage to hurt you.

BEN. Oh.

MAY. And all that time we would have continued to be strangers in a house [together.]

BEN. [Why are you] telling me all of this now?

MAY. Because you came here and saw me and because, okay, because I don't love you anymore, Ben.

       (Pause.)

BEN. May, I don't know how to be alone. You know I don't know how to do that. That's not a reason to stay, that's a terrible reason to stay, but I don't know what to do, the house will be so empty if it's [only me.]

MAY. [I said I don't] love you anymore and you're thinking about the empty house. You'll have to find something else that can hold your attention because I don't and I don't feel like anything does anymore.

BEN. How long have you been, I don't want to know. How long have you wanted to, I don't want to know that either.

MAY. Good.

BEN. When I saw your face, how disappointed you were that I couldn't come on this trip, I hated myself for sending you off alone.

MAY. That wasn't disappointment. That's not the face I made.

BEN. I know you well enough at this point [to know...]

MAY. [Fine, fine, that] was disappointment. Happy? I was disappointed that you didn't tell me sooner because I didn't know if Toby would be available at the last minute to join me on the trip.

BEN. Glad it worked out.

(She chuckles and toasts him.)

MAY. We don't have this connection you imagine.

BEN. What we have is a marriage, May.

MAY. The idea that I should stay with you even if I come to truly believe that there's something better for me out there is soul crushing. Don't you feel that?

BEN. It's a choice to be together, an adult choice. Not some childish, ephemeral thing.

MAY. Careful now.

BEN. No, I have some things to say. So far all I've heard from you is some cryptic bullshit about how people change and how we changed and that's not gonna cut it for me. If you care about me at all, if you ever did, try to make me understand.

MAY. The thing that was love turned into something else. It doesn't excuse the cheating; I'm not trying to excuse it.

BEN. Why not?

MAY. Because I don't feel like I have to, Ben.

BEN. Why not?!

MAY. I swear to God, even now you're not listening to me. But I don't know how to explain it any better. Sometimes it's okay to not know how to explain things. And I'm sorry, I don't know. Yet. But maybe one day I will?

BEN. Huh, so I have to wait around [for you to…]

MAY. [No, Ben,] you absolutely should not wait. You should move on and find something for yourself. And if one day we meet up somewhere for a nice lunch to reminisce and I've somehow figured out how to better explain what's happened to me, to us, then that will just be the icing on a piece of cake you finished a long time ago.

BEN. What if I don't show up for that lunch?

(Pause.)

MAY. I need to find Toby.

(She kisses **BEN** *on the cheek and slips away.* **BEN** *looks out the windows again for a moment. Then he comes back into the room, looks around, picks up the stuffed bear, lays down in the stain outline on the floor clutching it, filling his outline, so his hand is over* **AVERY**'s.)

*(***LINDA*** returns.)*

LINDA. I'm sorry to bother you, but I saw your wife and her, her "friend" in the hall and I wanted to check in on…

(She sees **BEN** *on the floor and slowly approaches.)*

Come on now, there's no reason to hide away in here. I surmise, well from what I witnessed, that this is a difficult time. But you can't just give up.

(Pause. She kneels down next to him.)

You have to get out there and find yourself again. Part of you is climbing out of that tidal pool at the base of the falls right now and starting over, living a completely new life. Making different choices. Being different.

(Pause.)

Maybe being happy. You saw him, didn't you?

(Pause.)

If you don't go find him, you'll just waste away and he'll go on without you. Don't be the part that's left behind. Trust me, it's nothing to embrace. I know. You'll just be haunted by the things that could have been. Haunted. Haunted.

*(***LINDA*** softly begins to sing **Dido's Lament (When I am laid in earth) by Henry Purcell**. It begins quietly but grows into a beautiful aria.)*

(As it grows, **AVERY** *gets up and moves away from the stain on the floor.* **LINDA** *rises and begins to drift away while still singing.)*

*(***AVERY*** goes to the windows and looks out. Suddenly,* **the tone sounds again, over the aria,**

bends into the discordant pitch and at its peak,
the sound abruptly stops with a jolt or a pop, also
ending the aria as LINDA *vanishes.* AVERY *sees*
something outside the windows that causes her to
shudder.)

(AVERY *begins to collect her purse, her sweater,*
she's heading out with purpose when JACK *enters,*
dressed. He practically has to fight to keep her in
the room.)

JACK. I'm ready to go.

AVERY. I'll be back, Jack. I shouldn't be long, [I think.]

JACK. [Where are] you going?

AVERY. I don't have time to explain.

JACK. Avery, Avery, calm down. What has [gotten into you?]

AVERY. [I'm calm, I am] calm; I just have [purpose.]

JACK. [You're not] calm, I thought we were going [to breakfast?]

AVERY. [I have to make] sure we made the right decision. That sounds, don't think about that too hard. I just don't want to be out there somewhere living another life.

JACK. That doesn't make any sense? Oh, whoa, is this a cold feet thing or some [kind of…?]

AVERY. [No, what?]

JACK. You're supposed to have cold feet before the wedding, not after you actually [get married.]

AVERY. [It's not cold] feet, there wasn't even time for cold feet. It's maybe insane, I'm maybe insane.

JACK. You're not insane.

AVERY. Okay, no? Okay, I was looking out the windows at the [waterfall and…]

JACK. [Did you drink] all of that champagne [yourself?]

AVERY. [I was looking] out the window and I saw myself go over the falls, not in a barrel, sometimes people are in barrels, and then in a flash all of these things, all of these things, a Ferris Wheel, a big Ferris Wheel, and another man, and a [different me.]

JACK. [Hold on,] another man?

AVERY. Not like that. Maybe like that, no, it was all such a jumble. And regret! There was regret and I didn't like that at all. This doesn't, listen, there is definitely something wrong with that stain.

JACK. Avery, baby, we can switch rooms if it's [still bothering...]

AVERY. [It has stories] in it or a story or somebody's, I don't know, I have to go.

> (**LINDA** *enters with her sleeves rolled up, awkwardly carrying two plastic buckets of soapy water and a scrub brush.*)

LINDA. I'm back to tackle that stain.

AVERY. Thank you.

JACK. Linda, that was your name, right? We're in the middle of something. Could you please come [back later?]

LINDA. [Oh, I'm] sorry.

AVERY. Don't apologize, Linda; you're just trying to help.

JACK. What?

LINDA. I do my best.

AVERY. And you have a beautiful voice.

LINDA. Oh, thank you?

JACK. Avery.

AVERY. I don't know why exactly you abandoned your dreams of singing opera, but it's never too late.

LINDA. Oh!

JACK. Who's even talking about opera?

AVERY. Linda told Ben. Isn't that right, Linda?

LINDA. I don't know [what you're...?]

AVERY. [Yes, yes, you] told Ben right before May and Toby came in and ruined the whole surprise, you remember.

LINDA. That's uncanny.

JACK. I don't know who any of those people are!

AVERY. Now where would I go?

JACK. I wasn't going to tell you this because of the "just say no" thing, but I have Xanax with me, a lot of Xanax, and I don't think it would be the worst thing in the world if you took one.

AVERY. I knew you had those.

JACK. You suspected I had them.

AVERY. No, I looked through your overnight kit when you were sleeping. It's a thing I do, nice to meet you.

JACK. What?

AVERY. And I don't need to take a pill, I need to find myself. Not figuratively, not in an introspective kind of way. I need to think about where I would be.

LINDA. And also you shouldn't take pills with champagne.

JACK. Thank you, Linda!

AVERY. The Ferris wheel, that's where I'd go. I'd go there all the time if I could. I'm probably there right now. Can I walk to the Ferris wheel from here?

LINDA. Yes.

AVERY. Yes?

LINDA. You just head down the boardwalk [until you…]

AVERY. [Perfect!] Where is my coat?

(She grabs her coat from a nearby chair or coat hanger.)

JACK. Okay, I'm not going anywhere until you tell me what is going on in your head.

AVERY. Then you stay here, that might be better. I love you, Jack.

JACK. I love you, too.

AVERY. Good.

*(**AVERY** leaves. **JACK** chases after her.)*

JACK. Avery, where are you going?

LINDA. Did you look out the windows too long? I bet you looked out the windows too long! I told you not to do that!

> (LINDA *exits, chasing after* AVERY *and* JACK *with the buckets of soapy water and brush.* BEN *remains motionless on the floor.* **The sound of the waterfall outside the hotel room** *begins to grow.*)
>
> (*blackout*)

End of Part One

Interval

*(The **Foley Ensemble** begins to sing or intone a slow dance song of some kind as a warm light slowly rises on the space. Cast members begin to remove all of the lingering set pieces from Part One. Even the white tape that marked the stain on the floor is pulled up (or eliminates it in some way, swept away, covered, etc.) Meanwhile, **AVERY** enters the space gingerly, followed by **JACK**. He takes her hand and they begin to dance to the music. A lovely slow dance. Something with structure and choreography, a repeated series of movements.)*

*(As the other cast members complete clearing the space, they couple up and join in the dance: **TOBY & MAY**, gracefully, and then **BEN & LINDA**, less gracefully.)*

*(As the interval continues, the live song thins out, dims, or just cuts out in some sort of sound shift, the same song rises as a recorded cue. Not the ensemble version, but whatever the original version of their song might be. Members of the **Foley Ensemble** rise one at a time, shed their rain ponchos, and join the dance. As they do, it becomes a group dance, no longer couples but still a series of choreographed processions.)*

(Strands of string lights of different colors, or isolated light bulbs, hanging around the space and above the actors shudder to life, warming the playing area. Transforming it.)

*(Once everyone is dancing, the group suddenly disperses. **AVERY** and **JANE** are left on stage for the*

briefest of moments. They glance at each other and then exit in opposite directions as the lights and the music shifts to become the ambient environment of a boardwalk carnival.)

(From this point forward, all sound cues in the show (with the exception of **BALE***'s mandolin) are pre-recorded cues as opposed to the Foley ensemble recreations from part one. The world is now different.)*

End of Interval

PART TWO

Fortunetellers & Daredevils

(The sounds of crowds fill the space, people milling about, chatting. On a screen of some kind, a shadow puppet of a rollercoaster appears. **BALE** *stands nearby smoking. He is wearing pants with suspenders; a short sleeve button-up shirt underneath is unbuttoned to reveal a white tank. He might even have a bowler hat. He has a mandolin at his feet and a big role of carnival tickets. His shoes, notably, have a high polish shine.)*

*(***MAX** *enters and stares up at the image of the rollercoaster. He's wearing a jacket, hands in his pockets. He looks nervous.)*

BALE. She's quite a coaster.

MAX. Uh huh.

BALE. Only takes three tickets.

MAX. I know.

BALE. You have three tickets?

MAX. They gave me plenty at the entrance.

BALE. Well head on up then and give her a shot.

*(***MAX** *just stares.)*

You know, I'm not supposed to be smoking, but no one really pays attention to me over in this corner. Terrible habit, I know.

*(***MAX** *continues to stare.* **BALE** *steps into* **MAX***'s line of vision.)*

BALE. I've seen you here before, haven't I?

MAX. Maybe.

BALE. I'm good with faces. Helps when you're a "carnie." Ah, that's short for carnival workers, carnival folk. It's a phrase people use a lot to imply something undesirable, but it's a unique lifestyle and I'm happy to own it. So then I have seen you here before?

MAX. Yes.

BALE. Sure, maybe with a girlfriend, right?

MAX. I don't...yes.

BALE. I knew it. Standing and looking. You know it's a lot more fun to actually get on and ride her than it is to just stare from a distance. That's true of most things though, am I right?

> (**BALE** *laughs at his own implication.* **MAX** *continues to stare.*)

To each his own, I suppose. Hoo! She's got you all scared and frozen up, huh? I've never seen anything quite like it.

> (**MAX** *suddenly screams and screams at the rollercoaster.* **BALE** *is shocked.* **MAX** *stops and shoves his hands back in his pockets.*)

Okay.

MAX. I hate that thing.

BALE. No point yelling at her like that, she can't hear you.

MAX. It's awful.

BALE. It's just a rollercoaster.

MAX. It's a big, rickety, wooden bullet of death.

BALE. That's quite an imagination you have there. As far as I know, no one's ever died on her and I know pretty far.

MAX. Dumb luck. I'm trying to work up my nerve.

BALE. To ride her?

MAX. To burn it down.

BALE. Now hold on there, champ. That doesn't sound like the best reason to be building up steam. Look, sometimes you just have to get on the rollercoaster.

MAX. I don't want to ride it.

BALE. Better than trying to burn her down.

MAX. I don't want to ride it. I want to burn it down. With my own hands.

BALE. With your own hands? I don't even know what that means. Listen, sometimes you just have to get on the rollercoaster.

MAX. You already said that.

BALE. Only advice I've got. That and don't waste your time on a woman who likes to dance. That's just a bunch of trouble in the making, if you ask me. My wife? Two left feet and happy as you like.

MAX. Is she a devastating, heartbreaking liar?

BALE. Whoa now.

MAX. Because if she's not then you don't have much to say to me.

BALE. Now, if you don't mind my saying so, you seem a little too depressed or, well, "out of sorts" to properly enjoy these attractions.

MAX. Enjoy? I think this rollercoaster, this one right here, is the reason my girlfriend left me. I wouldn't ride it with her. I was too afraid, made them stop the ride on the first hill. Fucking humiliating. And I think it was the tipping point, or the, the whatever that small thing is that unravels everything else.

BALE. Listen, what's your name?

MAX. Max.

BALE. Max, I can tell you're sad. Hell, people looking down from the top of the Ferris wheel could tell you're sad, but you need to cheer up. Because you're making me sad. And nervous. Now, I'm Bale. Bale Ring.

MAX. Bale Ring?

BALE. Named after the central ring used to raise big circus tents. My parents were carnies, too. And you know what they taught me?

MAX. How to make cotton candy?

BALE. Sometimes you just have to get on the rollercoaster.

MAX. There's a shocker.

BALE. Already said it's the only advice I have.

> *(He laughs at his own wit again.* **MAX** *smiles big and takes a plastic bottle of something and a lighter out of his pockets.)*

What do you have there?

MAX. Gasoline and a lighter.

BALE. Well, I don't think I like that at all.

> *(***MAX*** *starts laughing. He becomes almost chipper.)*

MAX. Hey now, we're just chatting. Right?

BALE. I'm sorry I didn't realize earlier that you were serious. Here I thought you were just having one of those, what's the, an existential crisis.

MAX. How do you even know [that term...?]

BALE. [Because I read] books and Kierkegaard is one of my favorite thinkers. You shouldn't look down your nose at folks just because they choose to amuse people for a living.

MAX. I wasn't [doing that.]

BALE. [There's a lot] to be said for giving people a laugh or a thrill. And while we're on the topic, you shouldn't assume your pain entitles you to take something away that many other people enjoy.

MAX. I sort of think you're biased.

BALE. And I sort of think you're on the verge of a psychotic break.

MAX. You don't even know me.

BALE. Healthy, well-adjusted people don't commit arson. At a carnival.

MAX. You're wrong; it really helps. It's fully one hundred percent healthy. Listen, I burned down the shitty little diner where she broke up with me over Eggs Benedict while the waitress watched. Helped. I burned down the used car dealership where she said I didn't stand up for myself when I bought our Saab. Helped.

BALE. A Saab? What happens when it needs service? Such a hassle. There aren't a lot of dealerships where [you can...]

MAX. [Then I tried to] burn the store where we got our cell phone plan that she said we were spending "way too much" on, but the fire alarm went off and I had to run.

BALE. You might actually be well past that psychotic break I mentioned.

(**MAX** *laughs even more.*)

MAX. It's really cathartic.

BALE. So is just getting on the rollercoaster.

(**MAX** *suddenly screams at the rollercoaster again.*)

Okay. We don't know each other, but eventually this is gonna catch up with you. And even if it doesn't, legally speaking, how is any of this making the fact that she's gone any better?

MAX. I don't like who that guy is. I don't like that guy, Bale. I can't be that guy. And every one of these places that burns down is one more piece of that guy she didn't love that's gone forever. And once he's all gone, completely gone, I'll be a different man.

(*Pause.*)

BALE. Is there...is there more?

MAX. That's it. We're nothing but our experiences, right? Erase those and start fresh. You'd be amazed, really. Amazed. It feels amazing.

BALE. Now I haven't gone to get the police, I haven't called for help, I've been really understanding, can you give me that much?

MAX. Okay.

BALE. Right, so I'm genuinely without an agenda when I say to you that is a really naïve thing you've convinced yourself to believe.

MAX. Fuck you, you don't know how much it hurts.

BALE. Fuck you, it doesn't matter how much it hurts.

MAX. Yes, it does!

BALE. It really, really doesn't.

MAX. And you're really, really bad at talking people back from the edge.

BALE. I'll do better: We're not just our experiences, that's stupid. And you're stupid for letting yourself buy it. Dummy. We are what we do based on those experiences, how we learn. For instance, and not to be too on the nose here, do we simply overcome our fears and ride the God damn rollercoaster or do we turn into completely unhinged firebugs and put innocent people at risk on a futile errand to erase our pasts? An effort that will be entirely unsuccessful because getting rid of physical places doesn't change her memory of all the ways you think she thinks you failed her. And it doesn't change yours either. Now look, I'm just a carnie and I married a woman who's easily impressed and doesn't dance, so ignore me if you like. Ignore me and burn down that rollercoaster. But if you're gonna go ahead with your selfish, pointless, really bad plan, at least wait until the carnival closes so you don't hurt anyone else while trying to make parts of yourself disappear that are always going to be there. Always.

    (Pause.)

Always.

    *(**MAX** starts to speak but doesn't come up with anything. He turns and screams at the rollercoaster. This time it's different. It's not rage. This time he falls apart at the end of it.)*

Okay.

MAX. I'm sorry.

BALE. Don't be sorry, what was your name again?

MAX. Max.

BALE. Right, yes, Max. Don't be sorry, Max. Just stop setting things on fire.

MAX. It's still scary.

BALE. It's supposed to be scary. That's the point.

MAX. And she isn't coming back.

BALE. I don't know, but it doesn't sound like it.

MAX. But just, I should get on it anyway.

BALE. Yep. Now. Right now. Well, you have to wait in line. There are a lot of people waiting to do the same thing as you.

> *(Suddenly, the lights and sound "bend" for a moment as* **AVERY** *storms through the scene, moving with purpose. She is followed by* **JACK.** *Then* **LINDA,** *still carrying the buckets of soapy water and brush,* **BEN,** *toting the stuffed bear with a red ribbon around its neck, and then* **MAY** *and* **TOBY,** *hand in hand. She has a balloon. He has cotton candy.)*

AVERY. Excuse me, where is the Ferris wheel? I can see it, but how do I actually get there?

BALE. You're not going to burn it down are you?

AVERY. I don't think so. But also, I don't really know.

JACK. Avery, where are we going?

BALE. Just keep heading straight down the boardwalk, you'll run right into it.

AVERY. Thanks.

JACK. Avery!

> *(***AVERY*** heads out followed by the entire group.* **MAX** *looks at* **BALE** *and then follows after them.)*

> *(The shadow of the rollercoaster fades as a shadow of a fortuneteller appears on the small screen.)*

> *(***ESSA*** sits in a chair looking bored and a little bit too relaxed. She isn't dressed like a fortuneteller, but she has a clear glass ball sitting in her lap.* **BALE** *stands off to the side somewhere, maybe leaning against a wall. He plays the mandolin, a quiet little tune, and doesn't really pay attention*

*to the scene. But the music continues through
underneath.* **CLIFF** *walks by and stops, looking
at the shadow projection of the fortuneteller.* **ESSA**
perks up.)

ESSA. Fortune?

CLIFF. Oh, no. I'm sorry, I don't believe in all of this stuff.

ESSA. You don't have to believe in it for it to be true.

CLIFF. I'm pretty sure you do.

ESSA. Then I'm pretty sure you're gonna be blindsided by
life. A lot.

(She relaxes back into a slouch.)

CLIFF. That's your best sales pitch?

ESSA. If you don't believe, then you don't believe. Your loss.

CLIFF. Again, you're not really selling me on this [very
well.]

ESSA. [Look, I'm just] filling in for my Aunt Ezmerelda.
"Ezmerelda the Unflappable and All-Seeing." She had
to take her cat the vet at the last minute because it ate
something weird.

CLIFF. Like a penny?

ESSA. No, like a pack of golf tees.

CLIFF. Yikes.

ESSA. Anyway, I'm filling in. If you're not interested, cut
me some slack and move on. I need to work.

CLIFF. So you can both see the future?

ESSA. This is not "twenty questions" about my life.

CLIFF. It's interesting that it'd be you and your aunt.

ESSA. It's a family thing, do you want me to read your
fortune or what?

CLIFF. Okay, jeez. How much is it?

ESSA. Ask yourself if you can really put a price on knowing
the future. Yes, you can. Fifteen dollars.

CLIFF. Steep.

ESSA. You look like an uptight, white collar, available
resources kind of guy.

CLIFF. I hope it's worth it.

ESSA. Right? So pony up the cash and Ezmerelda the Unflappable and All-Seeing will be so thrilled.

> (*He takes out his wallet, opens it, and hands her some money. She glances furtively and quickly at the inside of his wallet. He hands her some cash.*)

CLIFF. What about you, do you have a fancy name?

ESSA. Essa.

CLIFF. That's...less fancy.

ESSA. It's short for Vanessa and I don't need all the smoke and mirrors and preamble because I have skills. You believe I have skills...don't you, Clifford?

CLIFF. Well, I believe you were skilled enough to glance at my name on my driver's license while I was getting money out. And it's Cliff.

ESSA. Okay, wow, rude.

CLIFF. I'm sorry, but like I said, I don't really buy this kind of stuff.

ESSA. You mentioned.

CLIFF. I'm sure there are all kinds of things in the world that we can't account for, but I've certainly never run into any of them. And I seriously doubt it's gonna happen here at a boardwalk carnival.

ESSA. You were one of those kids that told everyone how the magic tricks happen, right? Ruined other people's birthday parties by being a know-it-all? Classy. Now pull up a chair and let's knock this out.

> (**CLIFF** *pulls up a nearby stool.*)

CLIFF. This work?

ESSA. I don't know, does that look like a chair?

CLIFF. I, huh, okay, I didn't see any [other chairs.]

ESSA. [It's fine,] it's a stool, but it's fine. Here we go.

CLIFF. You could really work on your salesmanship.

ESSA. You're still here, aren't you?

CLIFF. You're intriguing.

ESSA. I already have your money, now hush.

> (**ESSA** *gazes into the crystal ball. The lights dim and a hum fills the space. Suddenly it all cuts out and she gives him a look.*)

That's odd.

CLIFF. What?

ESSA. Give me your hand.

CLIFF. Which one.

ESSA. It doesn't, just give me one.

> (*She grabs his hand and examines the palm. Again the lights dim and the hum fills the space. Again it all cuts out abruptly.*)

That is so weird.

CLIFF. What is it?

> (**ESSA** *takes his money out and hands it back to him.*)

ESSA. Here. Take this. Good luck.

CLIFF. Are you kidding me?

ESSA. Take your money back.

CLIFF. No. Tell me what you saw.

ESSA. I can't read your fortune so you deserve a refund.

CLIFF. Okay, you are a complete scam artist. I'm supposed to freak out and offer to pay more, right? I'm not giving you any more money.

ESSA. I didn't see anything, and that's strange. So it doesn't matter if you offer me more money because I can't help you.

CLIFF. I'll pay more.

ESSA. You just said you wouldn't.

CLIFF. I know what I said.

ESSA. I don't want your money. Thank you and good night.

> (**ESSA** *drops his money on the ground.* **CLIFF** *gets up to leave, but he doesn't collect the money. She notices this and gets annoyed.*)

No, no, you have to take the money back.

CLIFF. I paid for a reading. I suppose you did something just now, so caveat emptor or whatever. I only came to this carnival because I was having a really shit day at work and I needed, like, a lark or something. You have any idea what an actuary does?

ESSA. Does this story end with you taking the money?

CLIFF. I look at charts and numbers and assess risk for an insurance company. It's not exciting. And the overhead light in my office flickers at a really odd interval that's driving me nuts. And now I have no future and I'll get some cotton candy and call it a night. Thank you.

ESSA. No, it's like a karmic thing, you have to take the money back or I have to finish what we started.

CLIFF. Finish telling me my fortune?

ESSA. Or else I'll have bad luck. Forever. It's in the amazingly awful fine print of having this gift.

CLIFF. Harsh.

ESSA. Are you, like, the king of saying obvious things?

CLIFF. Huh…sounds like you've got yourself a real problem.

ESSA. My problem is that you're not showing up on, listen, if you're not gonna take your money then just sit back down and let me see if I can figure this out. There has to be a reason it's so difficult to see you.

CLIFF. Maybe I don't want to know now.

ESSA. You said your life is boring and you're still standing here; I don't need a crystal ball to figure that one out. Now sit your ass down.

CLIFF. Okay, jeez.

ESSA. Who says that, who says "Jeez?"

CLIFF. It's colloquial.

ESSA. Whatever, I'm going to touch your face, don't freak out.

(CLIFF *sits back on the stool.* ESSA *stands in front of him. She places her hands on his cheeks and looks deep into his eyes. The lights dim. The*

*humming returns. Suddenly, still looking into his
eyes, the words begin to spill from her rapidly and
without pause...)*

You know that game little kids play, 'Doctor'? I know
you know that game. Well when I was young, I played
that game with a little boy named Kenny James, he
lived across the street in a house that was smaller than
ours. It was nice enough, just smaller, so I always had
this lingering feeling in the back of my mind that I was
somehow better than him. I didn't know that's what it
was at the time, but that's what it was, I was better than
him. He also liked me a lot, and that made me feel
special too, and maybe a little bit powerful. He would
come over for play dates, I really hate that term, and
we'd go down to the basement, because that was the
only place my Mom didn't circle above us like some
looming scavenger bird. It was like the basement was
a special place and Kenny was a special boy and all of
that, in our big house, made me special. I think I loved
Kenny. Well, the way a five year-old girl falls in love.
And I think I could see a future for us together, if I
closed my eyes, I could see all the way into the future,
so we would play 'Doctor' every weekend. Kenny was
happy to show me the basic logistics and I'm proud to
say that, even though it's not terribly complicated, I was
a quick learner and so this went on for a few months I
guess, you remember time funny when you think back
to childhood, right? But it went on for a while and one
day, kind of randomly at the bus stop, I heard some
of the other neighborhood girls talking. And giggling.
Turns out Kenny was playing 'Doctor' more than
I thought. In fact, he had a thriving practice on our
little cluster of streets. He was a regular with the house
calls. I remember all at once, nothing felt very special
anymore. And I was angry and hurt and confused and I
think that little scenario, well, it kind of officially set the
tone for my entire love life up 'til now.

(ESSA falls back into the chair, taxed and uncomfortable as the lights abruptly shift back and the humming stops.)

What in the hell [was that?]

CLIFF. [That was] amazing!

ESSA. What?

CLIFF. I felt like I was watching big pieces of your childhood. But all at once, in a flash, so I kinda had to piece them together.

ESSA. You don't just look inside someone!

CLIFF. It was like being pulled [into…]

ESSA. [It's not] supposed to work like that. And that's the past, not the future; things I don't even think [about anymore.]

CLIFF. [I didn't do] anything, I promise.

ESSA. Just…the only things that ever come up are relevant to, no, the fact that I don't trust men doesn't have [anything…]

CLIFF. [You don't trust men] because some little boy was playing doctor with other girls when you were barely old [enough to…]

ESSA. [That is none of] your business now please just forget you ever saw that, complete and total stranger.

(Pause. He eyes at the crystal ball.)

CLIFF. Did you see anything about me?

ESSA. No.

CLIFF. I never played Doctor with anyone, so maybe I don't [have the…]

ESSA. [Oh my] God, humiliation.

CLIFF. Can I see your crystal ball?

ESSA. No. It's a family heirloom.

CLIFF. Please.

ESSA. Why?

CLIFF. I can't explain it exactly, but I'm having this insane compulsion to hold the thing.

ESSA. It's good to learn to control your urges.

CLIFF. I'll be careful.

ESSA. Everyone wants to be a fortuneteller now, great.

> *(As she passes it to him, they're both touching it and the lights dim, the humming returns louder.)*

Now I see you.

> *(They both stare into the crystal ball.)*

Now I see you leaving here but feeling a tug and coming back, you come back to this place, to see me, to see me? Why me? You come back and take my hand and I'm afraid to go with you, but I do, something tells me I do, or maybe I saw it in your future now and I know I'm supposed to go even though I don't trust you yet and we walk through the lights and sounds, through all of the people, [we walk together away from this carnival and you kiss me under a broken sign for a Super 8 Motel and we have so many dinners and anniversaries and we get a dog named Marzipan even though you hate that name and when you ask me to marry you I almost choke to death on the peppermint candy in my mouth but you save me and you get old and I get old and you kiss that waitress in your car one night but you tell me about it and I understand that it doesn't mean the end only a little bit of hurt in exchange for so much love and I forgive you and we get even older together and at my mother's funeral Aunt Ezmerelda said she always knew it would be like this for us.]

CLIFF. [We walk together away from this carnival and I kiss you under a broken sign for a Super 8 Motel and we have so many dinners and anniversaries and we get a dog named Marzipan even though I hate that name and when I ask you to marry me you almost choke to death on the peppermint candy in your mouth but I save you and I get old and you get old and I kiss that waitress in my car one night but I tell me about it and you understand that it doesn't mean the end only a little bit of hurt in exchange for so much love and you

forgive me and we get even older together and at your
mother's funeral Aunt Ezmerelda said she always knew
it would be like this for us.]

>   (*They kiss. A massive, all consuming kiss. They
>   pull apart and look at each other. The lights return
>   to normal and the humming fades. Smiles.* **CLIFF**
>   *reaches out and gently takes her hand.*)

You're good at your job.

ESSA. I told you.

CLIFF. I mean…that was a lot.

ESSA. Right?

CLIFF. Whoa.

ESSA. It comes how it comes, sorry.

CLIFF. I suppose this is where I walk away so I can decide
to come back.

ESSA. And make your move.

CLIFF. If that's what you saw.

ESSA. I don't even know you. This is just plain crazy. But
that is what I saw. However… I don't know if you have
to go right this minute.

CLIFF. What would Aunt Ezmerelda say?

ESSA. Whatever. Her real name is Vicky and she knows
damn well how hard it is to find a good man.

>   (*Suddenly, the lights and sound "bend" for a
>   moment as* **AVERY** *storms through the scene,
>   moving with purpose. She is still followed by* **JACK**.
>   *Then* **LINDA**, *still carrying the buckets of soapy
>   water and brush,* **BEN**, *toting the stuffed bear
>   with a red ribbon around its neck, only the bear is
>   considerably larger now, and then* **MAY** *and* **TOBY**,
>   *holding hands. Now* **MAY** *has several balloons and*
>   **TOBY** *has even more cotton candy. Then* **MAX**
>   *crosses chasing after them.*)

>   (**CLIFF** *and* **ESSA** *exchange a curious look and
>   follow after them.* **CLIFF** *is carrying the crystal*

ball. **ESSA** *runs back on, picks up* **CLIFF**'s *money, and then rushes to catch up to the group.)*

(The shadow of the fortuneteller fades as a shadow of a Ferris wheel appears on the small screen.)

*(***BALE*** *sets down his Mandolin and crosses over to stand next to the image of the Ferris wheel.* **JANE** *and* **DAN** *enter. They hold hands as they walk.)*

JANE. Oh! We have to do the Ferris wheel. Come on, Dan. We have to.

DAN. It's just so boring. You just sit in a little car and go around in a circle.

JANE. It's romantic.

DAN. Jane.

JANE. It is, it's so romantic.

DAN. Okay, fine. Whatever. Let's go on the super exciting Ferris wheel.

(She kisses him.)

I mean, we can go on it as much as you want.

(She kisses him again.)

You're so easy.

JANE. I guess I really am.

(They begin to move forward, but **BALE** *also steps forward, arms crossed, to block their path.)*

BALE. Howdy, folks. Gonna need you to hold up.

JANE. Oh, we just want to go on the Ferris wheel.

BALE. Yep, sorry about that.

DAN. Look, pal, the lady just wants to go on the Ferris wheel.

(She shoots **DAN** *a look.)*

And me, too. I also want to, we both would like to go on the romantic, exciting Ferris wheel.

BALE. And that is a shame because it's out of service.

JANE. I can see people up there.

BALE. That's fair. And valid. And they've been stuck up there for over an hour now. We're working on it, well not "we." The mechanics are fixing it. I'm just standing here explaining to folks and I just can't tell you how long it'll be.

JANE. Oh no.

BALE. It is disappointing.

DAN. Thank God we weren't on it when it stopped working. Sounds like a mini-nightmare of really frustrating boredom.

JANE. We can't all jump ravines for a living.

DAN. Ravines? I've jumped exactly one ravine.

JANE. You know what I mean. Unless it's life or death, you don't think it's interesting.

DAN. Not fair.

*(She starts talking to **BALE**, but it's more of a performance.)*

JANE. Do you recognize my boyfriend? He's a daredevil. That's an actual profession. Can you believe that?

BALE. Well, I'm a carnie. So [that's...]

JANE. [When we] started dating, I thought to myself: "Jane, you're gonna always be worried for his safety. Don't you fall in love with a daredevil. Don't you do it."

DAN. Can we please spare this guy your theatrics?

JANE. But I try not to worry about him because he's good at what he does. So now I think: "Jane, why are disasters, plane crashes, and car accidents the only things that can hold this man's interest?"

BALE. Can he dance?

*(**JANE** turns to **DAN**.)*

JANE. Can you dance?

DAN. Yes. And you hold my interest more than any of those other things.

JANE. You can dance?

BALE. Trouble.

DAN. So this is a fun little performance.

JANE. We come here all the time, but he never takes me on this ride.

BALE. You do look familiar.

JANE. Mm hm. All the time. And I could go by myself, I suppose, but the idea of doing it alone is just so sad.

BALE. The cars are built for two.

DAN. Okay, okay, thank you, good sir, for the information about the Ferris wheel. We won't bother you anymore.

JANE. Fine. I just wanted to do something sweet together. That doesn't involve potential death.

DAN. This could involve death. The Ferris wheel. You could die of starvation up there. You could die of exposure. You could [die of...]

JANE. [Well we] don't have to ride it now, do we?

DAN. But I did want to ride it with you.

JANE. You just got done saying [that you didn't.]

DAN. [Because I know] how much you love to ride it.

JANE. Patronizing. Great.

DAN. No, I'm not [being...]

JANE. [Save it,] okay.

> *(He stops. He looks over at* **BALE** *who's really obviously listening.)*

DAN. Could you give us a minute, man?

BALE. I have to stand here; it's my job.

JANE. Sure.

DAN. Right.

> *(***DAN** *takes* **JANE** *by the hand and pulls her away from* **BALE**.*)

Are we, is this the beginning of a real argument or are you being cute?

JANE. I was being cute, but now I'm getting annoyed.

DAN. Me too. Because I don't think it's fair that you're bringing all this daredevil stuff up as, I don't know, like a passive aggressive [way to...]

JANE. [Hold up.] This "daredevil stuff" is your life.

DAN. No, it's my job. And it's not like you're some homebody. We met, for God's sake, we met in the intensive care unit.

JANE. And?

DAN. You went over Niagara Falls and survived.

JANE. Shut-up.

DAN. That's more insane than anything I've ever done. So calling me out for being an excitement junky, on a nice night, on a night that could be especially nice, is [really not...]

JANE. [Okay, okay, let's] just revisit this one more time as you seem really unclear on the facts: I went over the falls on accident. I accidently fell in the water, somehow, and accidently went over the raging waterfall, and barely survived crashing into that tidal pool. You on the other hand were there because you intentionally jumped off a bridge.

DAN. So you knew what you were getting.

JANE. Well, maybe I don't like it.

DAN. Since when?

JANE. It seems small right now, but it's not going to change, you're always going to be this way. And if you're not going to change and I'm not going to be okay with it then how are we [ever going to...]

DAN. [We'll figure] it out.

JANE. If that fucking Ferris wheel weren't broken then we [wouldn't even...]

DAN. [Just accept me for] who I am and know that I love you more than anyone ever has, ever will, forever.

JANE. Oh God, Dan, how can you talk in those grandiose, I mean it's sweet, but nobody really talks [that way.]

DAN. [Also, I don't] think my "lifestyle" is what you're really worried about.

JANE. It really is.

DAN. Nope.

JANE. It really, really is.

DAN. What's your name?

> *(Pause.* **JANE** *looks really surprised and angry.)*

Well?

JANE. Is this something we talk about in public?

DAN. What's your name?

JANE. Do you want to break up right now?

DAN. No.

JANE. Then fucking stop it.

DAN. What's your name?

JANE. Why are you being such a jackass?

BALE. Excuse me?

> *(They both turn on him.)*

I can still hear you, seeing as how you're not making any effort to be quiet, and I just wanted to ask: are you the "amnesia lady?"

JANE. No, I am not the "amnesia lady."

DAN. Yes, she is. Survived Niagara Falls with no memory at all.

JANE. Shut-up, Dan.

BALE. I saw your story on the news a while back. Just wanted to say that I'm glad you didn't die.

JANE. Are you fucking kidding me? You don't recognize him but you recognize me?

BALE. It's a memorable story.

JANE. You think that's fucking funny? "Memorable?"

DAN. She means, "Thank you."

JANE. I mean, "It's none of your business." Don't you tell him what I mean to say. Don't tell him anything, don't tell anyone anything. I know what my name is, it's Jane.

DAN. "Jane Doe."

JANE. That's what was on my hospital chart. Deal with it.

DAN. I've dealt with it.

JANE. Then why the fuck are you bringing it up?! I just wanted to go on the Ferris wheel, Jesus, and now I'm screaming in the middle of the carnival.

> *(Pause.* DAN *pulls a ring box out of his jacket pocket. Her eyes get huge and her mouth falls open.)*

No way!

DAN. I'm trying to make a point. Asking about your name, I'm trying to [make a point.]

JANE. [No, no, no,] no, no, no, no, no, [no, no, no.]

DAN. [Stop saying] "no" and listen to me, please.

JANE. I want to run away, so you better talk fast.

DAN. I don't care that you don't remember who you were before that accident, and I know that's hard to hear and hard for you, but I'm in love with who you are now. Not your story, not "amnesia lady." You, Jane, I'm in love with you. And every time I do a stunt, I still get terrified.

JANE. So do I.

DAN. But now I sort of invariably see my life flash before my eyes. Not in a scary way and I don't care how clichéd that sounds, it's true. It's totally true. And lately, it's been flashing a lot more of you then anything else. A lot more of you. Because you're right in the front, you're what matters most. To me. Whether we're having a caramel corn, slow dancing together, or arguing in front of a broken Ferris wheel. You.

> *(He opens the ring box. Her eyes light up. She's still uncertain, but definitely impressed.)*

I wanted to do this on the actual Ferris wheel.

JANE. Then why were you being such a dick about riding it?

DAN. I mean, I have this reputation to uphold.

JANE. It's a beautiful ring.

DAN. Good, it cost enough.

JANE. Oh, okay.

DAN. No, ugh, I shouldn't have said that. I'm kinda thrown by all of this. I know I'm the one asking, but I didn't think we'd be fighting. And I thought we'd be up in the air with lights and music and, I don't know.

BALE. Sorry again.

>   (**DAN** *shrugs.*)

DAN. But here we are.

JANE. Wait.

DAN. Jane.

JANE. I just need to say this.

DAN. Is it too much to hope you could just say "yes" first?

JANE. I totally know what you mean about seeing your life flash before your eyes. I know I don't talk about it, but the only thing I sort of remember from the accident, or incident, is going over the edge of the falls and seeing my life flash before my eyes. Something like my life.

DAN. You don't have to talk about it.

JANE. Yes, I do.

DAN. Okay.

JANE. I can't make sense of it, like a jumble of images and noise, but it was comforting. While my mouth full of water, falling, it was comforting. And even though it doesn't make any sense to me now, that life is still out there somewhere.

DAN. All right.

JANE. And it didn't include you.

DAN. You didn't know me then. That [doesn't count.]

JANE. [But it's a lot to] let go of if I'm going to really start something new.

DAN. If?

JANE. You know what I mean.

>   (*Pause.*)

DAN. So "if" you haven't let it go that means you haven't really started something new and here I am...

(He closes the ring box and pockets it.)

Making a fool of myself. Well, I guess I was never afraid to take a risk and fail big.

JANE. Don't think of it like that, please. I love you.

DAN. I love you, too.

JANE. I absolutely love you.

DAN. Okay.

JANE. I'm just scared of what might get left behind, you know?

DAN. So then you never get to move ahead? That can't be right.

(Suddenly, the lights and sound "bend" for a moment as AVERY storms into the scene. She is followed by JACK. Then LINDA, still carrying the buckets of soapy water and scrub brush, BEN, toting the stuffed bear with a red ribbon around its neck so large now that he has to drag it, and then MAY and TOBY, holding hands. MAY now has an enormous bundle of balloons and TOBY has more cotton candy than any person should. And then MAX, followed by CLIFF, with the crystal ball, and ESSA.)

JACK. Avery, you have to stop!

AVERY. I can't. It's just up ahead. We're almost...

(She stops when she sees JANE. And JANE stops when she sees AVERY. Everyone is now on stage. All of the lights dim for a moment except for a special on the two women and the strands of string lights. Then very quietly...)

AVERY & JANE. Oh my God.

(The lights return.)

JACK. [Avery?]

DAN. [Jane?]

AVERY & JANE. This is amazing.

JACK. [Look, it's just a Ferris wheel.]

DAN. [Do you know all these people?]

AVERY & JANE. Maybe.

JACK & DAN. Just tell me what's going on?

AVERY & JANE. Give me a minute.

> *(**JACK** and **DAN** notice **AVERY** and **JANE** look very similar.)*

JACK & DAN. Whoa.

AVERY. I saw you go over the falls.

JANE. Did you?

AVERY. From a window, high up, but I think it was you.

JANE. It was me, I think. But that was, that was a long time ago.

AVERY. No. Was it? We've been wandering around this carnival [for a while.]

JANE. [It's almost] surreal, isn't it?

> *(Pause. They touch hands tentatively. But when they do, the lights and sound undulate.)*

AVERY & JANE. Oh! Okay, this is so bizarre.

AVERY. I had to come and find you because we just got married and [I didn't know if it was the right thing to do.]

JANE. [You didn't know if it was the right thing to do.]

AVERY. I did it anyway, all so fast, but I still didn't know if it was right. And then there was this stain on the carpet with somebody else's story inside of it and it all just kind of crashed down on me.

JANE. Are you okay?

AVERY. I don't know.

JANE. He just asked me to marry him, sort of, and I don't know what to do either. Oh, that's Dan.

AVERY. That's Jack.

JACK & DAN. Hi.

JANE. So he asked me to marry him, but I don't know what to say to him [because I still remember the life you had before.]

AVERY. [Because you still remember the life I had before.]

JANE. Yes.

AVERY. Yes.

JANE. He was going to ask me on the Ferris wheel but it's broken.

AVERY. Oh no, that's disappointing.

TOBY. Hey! This is the moment I told you about, my friend. I'm up there right now, stuck, making all the wrong choices so I end up down here.

> (He playfully puts his arm around **BEN**. **BEN** shrugs it away, so he puts it around **MAY**, pulling her close.)

JANE. Anyway, It would have been beautiful I think. You?

AVERY. He asked me in bed. We were drunk. It could have been better.

JACK. Hey!

AVERY. Jack, it could have been better. Oh, but we do have the honeymoon suite at one of the overlook hotels.

JANE. That sounds beautiful.

AVERY. It is. Mostly. Except for the stain. Oh, but they brought champagne.

LINDA. (Waving from the group...) I brought champagne.

EVERYONE ELSE IN THE GROUP. Shhhh.

JANE. And it must be a breathtaking view of the falls.

AVERY. Oh, but you're not supposed to look at the falls for too long.

JANE. I've heard that.

AVERY. Something like this might happen.

JANE. Or you might fall in.

AVERY. Can you imagine?

JANE. I can, I can tell you all about it. But I'm okay now.

AVERY. Good.

AVERY & JANE. But there's two of us...does this mean we have to choose one?

> *(They each look over their shoulder.* **AVERY** *at* **JACK** *and the entire waiting group and* **JANE** *at* **DAN**.)

It looks that way.

JACK & DAN. What are you doing?

AVERY & JANE. This is where I ended up so it must at least be...

LINDA. This is so exciting.

EVERYONE IN THE GROUP. Shhhh!

AVERY & JANE. I choose this.

> *(The suddenly turn back towards each other in disagreement.)*

No, I choose this.

AVERY. I want to be with Jack.

JANE. I don't know who Jack is; I want to be with Dan.

AVERY. Dan doesn't look very put together.

JANE. He's amazing. And your guy looks shifty.

AVERY. Shifty?

JANE. We both know what I mean.

AVERY. He's not shifty. He's charming.

JANE. Charming?

AVERY. Yes. And he's a lot better than all of the other guys we've dated.

> *(***JANE*** leans in, genuinely curious...)*

JANE. How many guys?

AVERY. Enough. Don't ask me that in front of him.

JANE. Oh, no, I just have no idea.

AVERY. Besides, you haven't even talked to Jack. You don't know him.

JANE. I don't need to know him, you ran out on your own honeymoon.

AVERY. I mean, that's not fair. There was a stain and weird, I don't know, visions and what, like your guy is so different or so much better?

JANE. I don't know. Yes? I think so.

AVERY. Well it's too late, I'm already married.

> (*She holds up her ring finger and brandishes the hardware.*)

JANE. Dan, give me that.

> (**DAN** *quickly scrambles the ring box out of his pocket and hands it over. She opens it, pulls the ring out, and drops the box.*)

AVERY. Don't you dare.

> (*She slides the ring on her finger.*)

JANE. Now we both have a ring.

AVERY & JANE. Ugh, this doesn't feel right.

AVERY. I had to know if you were out here, but [I want my life.]

JANE. [I want my life] and it doesn't matter [if you don't approve.]

AVERY. [If you don't approve] of my choices then you can vanish or disappear or [go away and let me have this.]

JANE. [Go away and let me have this;] it doesn't matter if it's right because [it's what I choose!]

AVERY. [It's what I choose!]

> (*They turn to their respective men.*)

AVERY & JANE. Say you want to be with me forever.

JACK & DAN. I want to be with you forever.

AVERY & JANE. Say it's going to be okay.

JACK & DAN. It is going to be okay.

AVERY & JANE. Say you love me.

JACK & DAN. I love you.

AVERY & JANE. Say it again!

JACK & DAN. I love you.

> (**AVERY & JANE** *kiss* **JACK & DAN** *passionately. The assembled group begins to clap. The sound of rushing water, rapids and Niagara Falls, begins*

to rise. **AVERY** *and* **JANE**, *still holding on to their men, turn to face each other.)*

AVERY & JANE. Can we both have this?

(*The water gets louder.*)

I don't think we both get to have this. But this is what I want.

BALE. I've seen enough at this carnival to know that anything's possible.

AVERY & JANE. What?

(*The water becomes deafening.* **BALE** *shouts.*)

BALE. I said, anything's possible.

AVERY & JANE. I can't hear you over the water.

BALE. Anything's possible!

AVERY & JANE. What?!

BALE. Anything's possible!!

(**AVERY** *and* **JANE** *turn to look at each other as the sounds of rushing water entirely swallow the stage, burying it in crushing, deafening waves as the lights crash to a deep blue or black.*)

(*They almost immediately pulse back up in moving dim blues that restore to normal revealing* **AVERY** *and* **DAN**, *soaking wet, alone together on stage in front of the Ferris wheel projection.*)

DAN. Jane, are you okay?

AVERY. Yes.

DAN. What was that?

AVERY. I remember now.

DAN. And why are we all wet? I'm soaked.

AVERY. I remember everything. I remember everything!

DAN. Wait. Like, "everything" everything? Everything about [your life?]

AVERY. [Yes. Yes!]

DAN. That's [incredible.]

AVERY. [It's all there,] all of it!

> *(She leaps towards him and they hug. Suddenly she pulls away, mystified and overwhelmed by the information as it spills out...)*

Oh my God! Just like that, all of it. I had a pug named Matilda, my mother is super overbearing and wears the worst acrylic nails, and I can cook in a wok, and I like the poetry of Octavio Paz, oh, and Billy Collins too, and I can salt the sidewalk, why can I salt the sidewalk? Oh, because I grew up in Toronto! Wait, I'm Canadian. Holy shit, I'm Canadian. I'm a Maple Leaf! I might still have season tickets? And I like eating grapes at the supermarket without paying for them because it makes me feel like I have agency in the world, that's less than subtle, and clearly I have criminal tendencies, and I know how to do Sudoku, whoa, you know I hate Sudoku. But I guess I don't. But I do hate the texture of Avocado and the smell of Windex and foam mattresses and dead things, they scare me, and I hate wet plaster, and I love...

> *(Pause. The lights expand to reveal all of the other cast members in a group, intensely watching the scene unfold.)*

DAN. Oh.

AVERY. No, now, it's just still all a jumble [and I...]

DAN. [Well, we] always knew this could happen. Hoped for it even. And you've got a whole other life.

AVERY. Dan.

DAN. It's good.

AVERY. You don't have [to be...]

DAN. [No, now, I'm] not saying I like it. I'm saying I understand it. But I'm happy you know who you are again. Know what you want.

AVERY. I think I do.

DAN. Then I'm happy for you.

AVERY. I love you.

DAN. Good.

AVERY. I'm saying I love you. Specifically.

DAN. Eh, it was worth the risk, right?

> *(He smiles at her. He's doing his best.)*

AVERY. I swear, you can be the so bull headed sometimes, you're not listening. I love you, Dan. I remember everything and I still choose this. Maybe that's reckless, I don't know, but I choose you. And I'm not thinking about what could have been anymore. I'm not going to do that. I love you, Dan. Right now.

DAN. Right now.

AVERY. Yep.

DAN. Are you sure?

AVERY. Of course I'm, Dan, of course. I choose this.

DAN. I love you, Jane.

AVERY. Actually, it's Avery.

DAN. Avery. Avery?

AVERY. Avery.

DAN. Huh, I'm not gonna lie, that'll take some getting used to.

> *(They kiss. Passionately. The group of onlookers applauds, except **JACK** and **JANE**. There is a loud sound, like giant joints and bolts unlocking, metal creaking to life, and the shadow of the Ferris wheel begins to turn. Soft music rises.)*

BALE. Looks like we're back in business, folks! Who wants to ride?

End of Play

Lightning Source UK Ltd.
Milton Keynes UK
UKOW06f0818140815

256879UK00001B/8/P

9 780573 704581